BLOOD TIES

BLOOD TIES

Garth Nix and Sean Williams

SCHOLASTIC

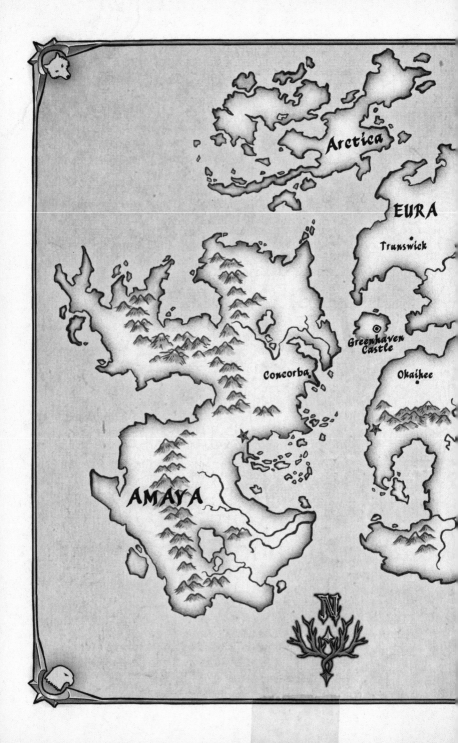

Arctica

EURA

Trunswick

Greenhaven
Castle

Okaihee

Concorba

AMAYA

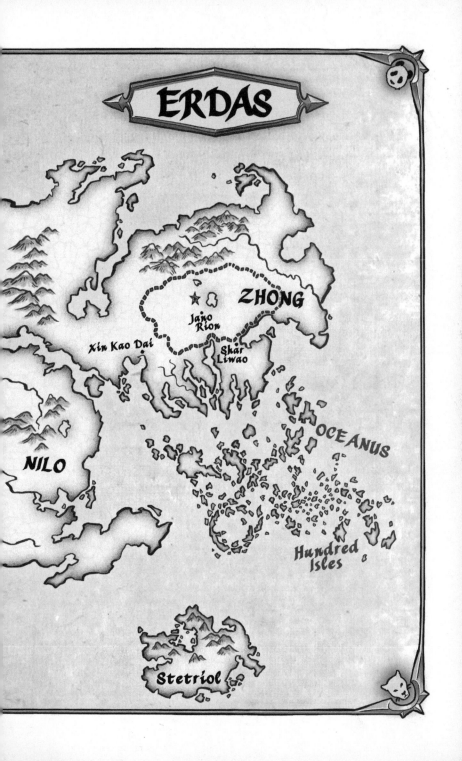

ERDAS

ZHONG

Jano
Rion

Xin Kao Dai

Shar
Liwao

OCEANUS

NILO

Hundred
Isles

Stetriol

For all the furred, feathered, finned, and scaled friends who have enriched my life.
— G.N.

For Skipper and Jumpy, the frogs who came to visit, their owner Amelia, and her twin brother, Orlando.
— S.W.

Scholastic Australia
345 Pacific Highway Lindfield NSW 2070
An imprint of Scholastic Australia Pty Limited
PO Box 579 Gosford NSW 2250
ABN 11 000 614 577
www.scholastic.com.au

Part of the Scholastic Group
Sydney • Auckland • New York • Toronto • London • Mexico City
• New Delhi • Hong Kong • Buenos Aires • Puerto Rico

First published by Scholastic Inc. in 2014.
This edition published by Scholastic Australia in 2014.
Copyright © 2014 by Scholastic Inc.
Map illustration by Michael Walton.
Book design by Charice Silverman.

ISBN 978 1 74362 000 7

Printed by McPherson's Printing Group, Maryborough, Victoria.
Scholastic Australia's policy, in association with McPherson's Printing Group,
is to use papers that are renewable and made efficiently from wood grown in
sustainable forests, so as to minimise its environmental footprint.

10 9 8 7 6 5 4 3 2 1   14 15 16 17 18 / 1

1

THE GREAT BAMBOO MAZE

THE BAMBOO ROSE ABOVE MEILIN, FAR ABOVE, BLOCKING out the sun and casting deep shadows on the intersection of two narrow paths below. Meilin stopped and glared at yet another crossroad in the Great Bamboo Maze, yet another choice of ways. She did not want to admit, not even to herself, that she had gone wrong somewhere several miles back and was now hopelessly lost.

It had seemed like such a good idea when she first thought of reaching Zhong through the Maze. The bamboo forest had been specially grown as a defense where the Wall did not run, and only selected messengers and senior officials knew the secret ways through the miles and miles of fifty-foot-high bamboo. Meilin's father, General Teng, knew the secrets, of course, and long ago he had told Meilin how to get through from the Northern Entrance.

"Always turn left the first ten times," whispered Meilin

to herself. "Then ten turns always right, then left, right, left, left, left, left, right, right, right."

But she had followed those instructions and had *not* found herself on the other side of the Maze. Even worse, she had counted on getting through in the single day it was supposed to take. The leather bottle of water she had filled from a stream at the entrance, plus two rice cakes should have been easily enough to sustain her.

Now it was the morning of the third day. Her water bottle was empty and the rice cakes were distant memories. This, coming at the end of a week's long trek by boat and caravan across Eura, often smuggled away in dusty crates and rat-infested holds, left her feeling frustrated at her failure, as well as hungry and thirsty. Only the distant hope that her father might still be alive, and that she might somehow live long enough to find him, kept her from giving up.

Angrily, Meilin struck the stem of the nearest bamboo with her quarterstaff, the blow so powerful that it cracked the four-inch-thick bole. The bamboo fell among its fellows, but there were so many it might never have been there in the first place. There was nothing but impossibly tall bamboo all around, the narrow path, the sun high above.

For the first time, Meilin thought she might actually die in the Maze. The daughter of General Teng, to die of thirst in a bamboo forest! It was unbearable!

An itch on her forearm diverted Meilin's thoughts. She slid up her sleeve and looked at the tattoo of a sleepy panda. She had kept her spirit animal, Jhi, in her dormant state in the Great Bamboo Maze, fearing the panda would hold her back. Now that was the least of Meilin's concerns.

"Come on, then!" ordered Meilin. "Come out and do

something useful. Maybe you could *eat* a way through the bamboo for me!"

There was a flash of light and sudden movement. A furry weight pressed into her side as Jhi appeared and leaned against her, pushing her against the closest stand of bamboo, making it shake.

"Hey, watch it," protested Meilin. She felt something touch her face, and thinking it an insect, brushed it aside, only to feel more of whatever it was land on her hand. She looked up and saw delicate white flowers falling from the tips of the bamboo high above, like tiny warm snowflakes.

Bamboo flowers.

Meilin had never seen bamboo flowers before. She knew the plants only flowered once every fifty or sixty or even a hundred years, and then they died. All the bamboo plants, all at once.

"The Maze is dying," she whispered, staring up at the tops of the bamboo. Every stand of bamboo she could see was flowering. In a week or two, the bamboo would begin to dry out, crack, and fall. Before that, the floor of the forest would be covered in flowers, attracting great hordes of rats and other animals to this once-in-a-century feast.

With the Maze gone, yet more of Zhong would be completely unprotected. The Conquerors had overrun her poor country through the Wall, and now even its lesser defenses were being torn away. Perhaps even this flowering had been caused by the Devourer somehow.

Jhi sat down heavily and reached up to drag Meilin down next to her with one big paw.

"I can't sit down!" protested Meilin. "I have to find a way out!"

She pushed the panda's paw aside and took a few steps along the left-hand path. Then she hesitated, turned, and took a few steps along the right-hand path. Jhi made a kind of snuffling noise.

"Are you laughing?" demanded Meilin. "This is very serious! I'm lost. I have no food or water. I could die here!"

Jhi patted the ground next to her. It was a very human gesture, and it reminded Meilin of her father, when he wanted her to sit next to him and receive some wisdom. What she wouldn't have given to see him now.

"I haven't got time to sit down!" she rasped. "Come on!"

It really didn't matter *what* path she took now, Meilin thought. She was totally lost. What was important now was speed. She had to get out of the Maze before she died of starvation and thirst.

She set off at a loping run, sure that this time there would be an opening in the tight ranks of bamboo, that the path would lead to a clearing, that she would be in the open lands of Zhong.

Jhi made another noise behind her, but Meilin ignored it. Once again, her spirit animal was proving useless. If only she had Essix! The falcon could fly up and spot the way out.

"You would think a panda might be of *some* use in a bamboo forest!" muttered Meilin. She ran on another fifty yards, and came to yet another intersection of paths. She could go left, right, or straight ahead. They all looked exactly the same: long narrow tracks between great stands of bamboo.

Meilin stopped and looked back. Jhi was following her slowly but steadfastly. As the girl looked, the panda reached up and pulled down a bamboo stem, effortlessly bending it until it broke. The topmost stems came down near the path just behind the girl, showering her once again with flowers. Jhi sauntered along and began to eat, stuffing huge pawfuls of bamboo stems, leaves, and flowers into her mouth.

Meilin felt her own hunger, a pain in her middle that was difficult to ignore. Her mouth would have watered, but it was too dry. She had tried eating the bamboo on the second day, and it had caused stomach cramps that only made her feel hungrier. It was too dry, and there were no soft, new shoots that would have been easier to digest.

"There has to be a way out," she whispered. She looked wildly at the different paths. There really was no difference between them. She had gone right last time. Now she would go left, Meilin thought. Left and then right at the next intersection, and so on. Zigzagging. That would work. She would get *somewhere* that way.

"Come on," she said to Jhi.

This time Meilin didn't run. She just didn't have the energy anymore. But she walked fast, ignoring her hunger pains and rasping throat, the heat and the humidity.

"I *will* find a way out," she whispered. "I *will* get to Zhong. I *will* fight the Devourer and our enemies."

But against that, there was a small voice in her head that whispered a hopeless, constantly repeating thought.

I'm going to die. I'm lost and I'm going to die.

2

A MESSAGE FROM
THE SEA

CONOR HUNCHED DOWN IN THE FOREPEAK OF THE *Tellun's Pride*, the fastest ship in the Greencloak fleet. He was drenched with spray every minute or so as the ship crashed through each rolling wave, but at least he could be alone in his misery. Being wet just felt like a small, suitable punishment for what he had done. Giving up the Iron Boar Talisman of Rumfuss to the enemy . . . even though he still felt like he had no choice, he had to do it to save his family . . . Conor felt hopeless and ashamed.

Not for the first time, Conor wondered if there had been some kind of cosmic mistake. Surely he was meant to be a shepherd and nothing more? He shouldn't be a Greencloak, and he shouldn't have one of the Great Beasts as his spirit animal. He just wasn't cut out to be a hero, and Erdas needed *real* heroes to obtain the talismans of the Great Beasts and defeat the Devourer.

Sharp teeth gently touched the back of his neck. He

knew those teeth. It was Briggan, grabbing him by the collar to pull him out of his hidey-hole, as if he were an errant cub.

"I'm coming, I'm coming," he said with a sigh.

The wolf let him go and backed up along the deck.

"What is it?"

Briggan turned and went toward the ladder down from the forecastle to the main deck, his claws clattering. At the top of the ladder, he looked back, his piercing blue eyes on Conor.

Conor looked past the wolf. Tarik, Rollan, and Abeke were standing facing each other just behind the mainmast, in a semicircle that had two obvious gaps. At least they were obvious to him. One was his own place, and he supposed Briggan had come to drag him there. The other empty spot was Meilin's. Meilin, who would never have gone off all alone to Zhong if Conor hadn't given in to the Earl of Trunswick and ruined everything. . . .

He considered his companions for a moment. Tarik really was a hero already, their mentor and guide, an experienced older Greencloak. Next to him, with that typical grin on his face, was Rollan, the smart-mouthed city boy. He didn't look like he was paying attention to Tarik, unlike Abeke. She was serious, she liked to do things properly, but she had been kinder to Conor than the others after he had failed them. Perhaps her calm center came from being a hunter. Abeke was patient with people as well as animals. . . .

"Ah, Conor! Come and join us!" called out Tarik. "We're going to try scaling the mast again, using Arax's talisman. You can go first."

"I thought it was Abeke's turn to go first," said Rollan with a thinly veiled glance of contempt at Conor. Conor winced. He'd once thought Rollan a friend, but not anymore. Not since Meilin left . . .

"Yes, it's Abeke's turn," Conor said. "She's better at jumping than I am anyway."

"That's why we practice," said Tarik patiently. "You'll need all your skills when we go after the next talisman."

"What is the next talisman?" said Abeke. "We don't know where another one is."

"And even if we get it," said Rollan, "Conor will probably just give it to the Conquerors anyway!"

"Enough of that!" said Tarik. "I am sure there will be news of one of the other Great Beasts when we get back to Greenhaven. Lenori will have found one for sure."

"I *am* sorry," said Conor, hating the way Rollan wouldn't meet his eye. "You know I am . . . but my family . . ."

"You people and your families," muttered Rollan. "It almost makes me glad mine ditched me early."

"The people we love are our strengths," said Abeke, "but they are our weakness too. When their lives are at stake, it is hard to know what is right."

The concession seemed to surprise Rollan as much as it surprised Conor. "You're letting him off the hook—?"

"I say only that we should try to understand." Abeke's glare was for both of them. "All lives are in danger until the Conquerors are defeated. All families, including my own."

That was a rebuke, one Conor felt he deserved. He bit his lip and reached for Briggan and the reassurance of the wolf's furry neck. But his fingers met empty air. Briggan had moved away. Maybe it was just because the ship had met another wave, bigger than usual, but it felt to Conor as if even his spirit animal didn't want to be associated with him too closely.

"Abeke's right," said Tarik. He spoke calmly, as always, but with considerable force. "Hence the importance of training. Here is the talisman. See how quickly you can reach the maintop."

"With Uraza's help?" asked Abeke. Her leopard was dormant, a tattoo on her forearm. Uraza was not keen on the sea.

Tarik shook his head. "Not this time. See what you can do just jumping with the talisman."

Abeke nodded. Conor looked up, worried for her. The maintop was a small platform only ten feet short of the mainmast's imposing eighty-foot height. It was reached by climbing up the ratlines, narrow nets of ropelike ladders that ran up from the deck. But what they had been practicing was jumping straight from the deck to the first spar, or crosspiece, that went across the mast. This was thirty feet from the deck. It was made even more difficult by the plunging and rolling of the ship.

If Abeke fell, Conor hoped she would try to aim for the sea. Better to fall in the water than be smashed on the deck—unless she landed on one of the rockback whales pulling the ship, of course.

"Focus," Tarik told her. "Concentrate on drawing the talisman's power. Aim for the exact spot you want on the spar, and have your hands ready to take hold when you land."

Abeke stretched her shoulders, then her calves. Uraza

was astonishingly dexterous, able to change direction even in midair. Conor didn't know how Abeke would fare without her.

"Go!" said Tarik as the ship settled down in the trough on the far side of a wave.

Abeke jumped. The astonishing power of the Granite Ram propelled her upward with thrilling acceleration. She was headed straight up, like a perfectly shot arrow – and then Conor realized that she was going too fast, jumping *too* high. She was going to hurl way past the first spar. In fact, she was going to go over the top of the mast, miss all the ropes, the spars, everything, and go plummeting down the other side!

Conor gasped as she desperately tucked in her knees and did a somersault in the air to slow herself down. Then, just as she cleared the very top of the mast, she stretched out, reached across, and gripped the thin rope there, the flag halyard used for raising the standard of the Greencloaks, guardians of Erdas. For a second Conor thought it might break, and he would watch Abeke go hurtling on her way to certain death.

But the rope held. Abeke swung around the mast and struck her shins against a horizontal spar. Her grip slipped a yard down the rope before she caught herself, swinging back the other way. The same wooden spar almost cracked her across the head. She avoided it only by executing an inelegant but effective somersault and kicking her feet against the spar. Finally she slowed enough to climb *down* to the maintop. There, she looked back to the deck seventy feet below. She waved, and Conor waved back with relief.

"That's one powerful talisman," said Rollan.

"It responds to Abeke's natural gifts," said Tarik, nodding in approval.

"I guess so," said Rollan. "Hard to see what use a wolf will be up there, eh, Conor?"

Before Conor could decide if that was supposed to be a joke or not, Rollan looked up. Essix, who had taken to perching on one of the stays that supported the mainmast, suddenly launched into the air with a long, falling cry.

"Has she seen something?" Conor asked.

Rollan pointed off to port, across the white-touched blue sea, toward the curved horizon. "There. A bird, I think."

Tarik was shielding his eyes with his hand and looking as well. "I can't see anything."

"Yes, a little black-and-white bird, flying low," Rollan went on. "It's kind of skipping over the waves, coming straight for us. Essix can't be hungry, can she? I fed her this morning!"

"It's a stormy petrel," said Tarik. "A messenger bird, like the pigeons of Eura. From Olvan or Lenori, I would guess."

A thud on the deck behind them made everyone turn. Abeke was there, crouched on one knee, one hand on the deck.

"I climbed down and then jumped from the lowest spar!" she said excitedly. "I knew I could do it. The talisman slowed me as I fell, like a feather drifting. Who's up next?"

"I think we'll take a break," said Tarik. "We have a message."

"I heard a song about stormy petrels once," said Rollan guardedly. "Don't they bring storms or bad luck?"

Conor, who had been straining to see, finally made

out a little bird rising up from the sea. It looked like it was bouncing off a wave. The petrel paused on the rail, then skittered to Tarik's hand. Essix flew overhead and landed on Rollan's shoulder, fierce amber eyes meeting the petrel's darting black ones.

Tarik carefully removed a tiny bronze capsule from the petrel's leg, and held the bird up. It made a squeaking, chattering sound and flew back to the open sea.

"There's a message in there?" asked Conor. "It looks too small."

Tarik nodded and twisted the tiny capsule apart. Inside was a scroll the size of his little fingernail. He took it out and unfurled it to a surprising length.

"Onion-skin paper," he said.

"Is it about Meilin?" asked Conor. He really hoped she was all right. They had been on a scouting mission for a week, to take their minds off the missing girl as well as to train them in seacraft. It hadn't worked. If only there was good news, that she was safe in Zhong with the Greencloaks there, or returning safely to them even now . . .

"In part," said Tarik. "It is from Olvan. '*No news of Meilin. Positive report on location of Dinesh. New orders. Go to Kho Kensit. Rendezvous messenger at Inn of the Bright Moon, outside East Gate of Xin Kao Dai. But beware. Enemy holds city. Good luck.*'"

"*Where* now?" asked Rollan. "I thought we were going back to Greenhaven, or at least somewhere warm."

"Kho Kensit is an outlying region of Zhong," said Tarik. Lumeo, his spirit animal, mimicked his frown, his little otter face all scrunched up. "Xin Kao Dai is the closest port."

12

"We can't just sail into enemy territory," said Conor. "We'd need an army!"

"It's a busy port, with travelers from all over," said Tarik. "If we disguise ourselves and get put ashore at night in one of the ship's boats . . ."

"I'm good with disguises," said Rollan. "There's a clothing box in the first mate's cabin. There's bound to be some cloaks that aren't green, plus other stuff we can use. Hey, we could dress up as minstrels! They always seem to come and go without any problems."

"We don't have any instruments," said Tarik. "Nor the skill to play them."

"What about shadow puppets?" suggested Conor. "A troupe visited Trunswick once. We'd only need a big sheet – we could borrow a sail – cut out some figures and get a big lantern. The troupe I saw did a show about all the different kinds of sheep, you know: Amayan Blackbelly, Euran Longhaired White. . . ."

"Sheep puppets!" exclaimed Rollan, as though he'd never heard anything more ridiculous.

"We will have a day to think of something, with the whales at full stretch," Tarik said. "I'll ask the captain when I inform him of the course change. He may have an idea we haven't thought of."

Abeke was rereading the message.

"Dinesh is the elephant, isn't he?" she said, pointing at the tiny script. "I mean *the* Elephant. The Great Beast."

"Yes," said Tarik. "Keeper of the Slate Elephant Talisman. Which we must obtain."

Abeke looked at Conor.

"We'll keep this one when we get it, right?" said Rollan.

Conor nodded miserably.

"Of course we will," said Tarik. "But for now, you should resume your practice, while the sea is relatively calm. Who's next?"

"You go," blurted Conor to Rollan. "I . . . I feel a bit seasick suddenly. I have to go lie down."

He turned and stumbled away, almost falling over Briggan before dragging himself alongside the rail to the aft companionway, and then down to the cabins below. The wolf patiently followed at his heels.

Conor didn't really feel seasick. He just felt ashamed. How could he practice when it was clear Rollan didn't trust him? Tarik and Abeke were trying, he could tell, but not Rollan. Every time Conor said something, Rollan was quick to put him back in his place. How could he help get a new talisman from another Great Beast when Rollan wouldn't let him forget how horribly wrong everything had gone with the Iron Boar?

Adding to his misery was the thought of sneaking into occupied territory, one of a handful of people against the full might of the Conquerors. Conor wasn't a coward, but what might happen if they were caught was too horrible to contemplate. He wasn't just worried about himself, but about Briggan too, and the people he had come to think of as friends, no matter what they thought of him. They would all have to contribute. There wouldn't be room for mistakes.

"I'll do whatever it takes," he whispered to Briggan as he sat on his narrow bunk and drew the wolf close. "I'll show them I can be a real Greencloak!"

3

XIN KAO DAI

X IN KAO DAI," THE CAPTAIN OF THE *TELLUN'S PRIDE* had said. "A pretty harbor, but prone to morning fogs this time of year. There's a small island very near the southern headland. We can stand off after midnight, row you to the island, and you can wade ashore at low tide. Cross the fish traps and you'll make landfall easily in the fisherfolk's part of the city."

Thinking of the captain's words two mornings later, Rollan wished they'd come up with a plan that didn't involve getting so wretchedly *wet*.

Captain Darish had been right about the fog. It wove around Rollan, thick and gray, shrouding the first faint rays of the sun. He wasn't cold, which was a surprise. He'd never encountered a warm fog before. But that didn't make him any less uncomfortable. The moisture was always pooling into droplets that trickled down the back of his neck and into his ears. When it dripped into his eyes, he had to blink and shake his head to fling the droplets away.

The sea was also warm, a detail that Rollan told himself to be glad of, since he was in it up to his waist.

"Whose great idea was this, anyway?" he muttered, doing his best to keep up with Tarik. Conor was following Rollan, and Abeke brought up the rear. All four of them had large shadow puppets strapped in bundles across their backs, the pieces of bodies and limbs poking above their heads and out to the sides. Tarik carried a great storm lantern strapped atop his pack.

The idea of telling the story of the Fallen had been Abeke's. She had described seeing such performances in Nilo, one with a Gerathon that had been made of no less than thirty segments, able to writhe and slide and open its mouth to devour everything in its path.

That detail hadn't thrilled Tarik.

The screen was by far the heaviest single piece, and Conor had volunteered to carry it, perhaps hoping it would make the others think better of him. Rollan didn't really understand why the shepherd had handed over the talisman to the Conquerors, since he didn't have a family himself. He didn't get why Meilin had chosen to run off either, to save someone who might already be dead, for all she knew. None of it made any sense at all to Rollan, who was just trying to keep his head above water, metaphorically as well as literally, at that moment.

"How far to the mainland?" he asked Tarik, keeping his voice low so it didn't carry across the water. The fog was so thick that he could only see a few paces ahead. They were all nervous about creeping into Zhong, where one mistake could leave them captives of the Conquerors.

But on the other hand, Meilin was in Zhong. Somewhere.

Rollan frowned as he found himself wondering where she was, and how soon he might see her again. He shook his head, trying to make the picture of Meilin in his head go away. This was no time to be thinking about someone who had chosen to run off and leave him . . . or . . . leave them.

"Are you all right?" asked Conor.

"Water in my ear," growled Rollan.

"Almost there," said Tarik. "I can see fish traps ahead."

"Are they dangerous?" Rollan had never seen one.

"Only to fish."

"You sure?" he said. "That'd be almost too eas–"

His right foot sank deep into an underwater hole and suddenly the surface of the sea came a lot closer to neck level than he liked. Splashing and spluttering, he barely managed to avoid falling face-forward, and was only hauled upright by strong hands from behind him. Conor.

"Are you all right?" Abeke's voice called from farther back.

Rollan pulled away from Conor.

"Can everybody stop asking if I'm all right? I'm fine."

He was fine, now that he had both feet back on the sea-bed. Annoyed, but not hurt in any way. Rollan knew he should thank Conor for helping him, but everything was too raw and complicated. All he wanted was to get out of the water and onto dry land, where he could run from the things that tried to hurt him, instead of splashing along at a painfully slow pace.

But at least he'd stopped thinking about Meilin.

"We must keep moving," said Tarik. "We need to be ashore and past the fisherfolk's huts before the fog lifts."

The Greencloak set a much quicker pace, and Rollan

struggled to keep up, now wary of invisible sinkholes. And fish traps.

"Remember, keep your sleeves down and tied at the wrist to hide your tattoos," Tarik said. "Call your spirit animals only if it is a matter of life or death. Obviously, this doesn't include you, Rollan. Hunting birds are common here, but I doubt normal for a troupe of puppeteers, so if Essix will stay aloft . . ."

Rollan wasn't promising anything. He was still embarrassed that he couldn't get Essix to adopt the dormant form. But at least the falcon could fly around without attracting attention. She was up there somewhere now, above the fog.

The fish traps turned out to be man-high, wickerwork tubes set into the sand. There were dozens of them, placed only a few feet apart so they formed a kind of strange forest emerging from the sea. Tarik led the way between the traps, which were full of flopping silver fish that had entered on the high tide and now couldn't get out.

The others followed him, moving faster as they waded steadily into shallower water. Soon they left the sea itself behind, dripping and splashing as quietly as they could.

The light was rising as the sun threatened to breach the eastern horizon. Through the muddy light Rollan made out a gently sloping, sandy beach, lined with drawn-up fishing boats. Behind the boats, a few dark outlines of houses could be seen through the fog.

There was a taller structure to their left, at the other end of the beach. A watchtower, fortunately still heavily shrouded by fog, so that only its lower wall was visible, and the faint red glow from the torches burning.

Tarik waved them on. They were painfully exposed on the beach. Hurrying up the sand, they followed a track that led to a line of fisherfolk's houses. If they weren't under cover by the time the sun burned the mist away, they'd be out of the fish traps and into a prison cell.

Upon reaching the houses, Tarik changed direction suddenly, leaving the track to hurry along behind a wall. The others went with him, Abeke only just reaching the shadowed wall as three fisherfolk came out of the swirling fog and started down to the beach with baskets on their backs and fish spears in their hands.

Red-tinged light spread through the fog. At the same time, Rollan had a momentary vision of the sun, a bright sliver of it above the horizon. He was seeing it from somewhere above the mist, through eyes much keener than his. He blinked and realized with a shock that the image had come from Essix.

He was seeing through the falcon's eyes!

Rollan's jaw dropped open, unfortunately just in time to catch a passing fly. He spat it out, hardly noticing because he was so amazed at what had just happened.

He had seen what Essix was seeing!

Rollan wanted to tell everyone. But it wasn't the right time. The sun was higher than expected; they were running later than they had planned. The working day of the city was about to begin. They had to get out of the fisherfolk's village and into the city proper before it was too late to merge with the crowd.

"We've got to move," Rollan whispered to Tarik. "Now!"

"Maybe we should try to hide until nightfall," said Conor nervously. "If everyone goes out fishing, the houses will all be empty."

"That's a terrible idea," Rollan snapped. "Families stay behind. And there might be patrols. We have to go now! The sun is up and it'll burn off this fog really fast."

"Rollan's right," said Tarik. He looked around. "If we can move between the houses, perhaps we can stay out of sight. The next quarter is a market. If we can get there . . ."

"Right," said Rollan, taking charge. He wasn't going to wait around for any more of Conor's hopeless ideas. "Follow me."

"Wait," said Tarik, gripping Rollan's shoulder before he could move out. "I'll go first. If we are seen by guards, you three can break off and run to safety."

"Not going to happen," Rollan said firmly. "No offense, Tarik, but even without your green cloak, you still stand out. Hang back and pretend to be our bodyguard or something."

Tarik lifted one shoulder and jutted out his jaw, simultaneously ducking his head and affecting a limp, taking on the perfect appearance of a brute. Rollan wondered if Tarik had more street smarts than he had given him credit for.

Rollan nodded approvingly. He listened for a moment, then started off along the back of the house, the others following. All his senses were alert, and he felt very alive. It was good to be back in a city, even on the fringe of one he didn't know. He would show the others what he could do, starting by getting into the market quarter.

He led the way behind four more simple wooden houses, and then a quick sprint through the fog to a line of posts where nets were hung for repair. Crawling under the suspended nets gave them perfect cover for a good twenty yards of easy travel. But then even Rollan was stumped. He held up his hand to halt everyone, and stared ahead.

The fog was really clearing now. With the increased visibility, Rollan saw there was a broad road ahead, separating the fishing village from the market stalls. People were already getting out their wares and exchanging shouted greetings about the fog.

But right in the middle of the road, there were two guards, a man and a woman. They looked like typical city militia to Rollan, in their badly kept leathers and dented helmets. But the woman had a spirit animal next to her, some kind of stoat, and that was not normal for a simple city guard. She had to be one of the Devourer's followers, one of the Conquerors who had taken over Xin Kao Dai.

"What do we do now?" whispered Conor.

Rollan held an impatient finger to his lips. That stoat might give the guard superior hearing, or it might notice them itself. He was thinking furiously.

Abeke mimed shooting an arrow. Her bow and quiver of arrows were underneath the shadow puppets.

Rollan shook his head. Shooting guards in a city? That was a sure way to get caught. They had to be distracted somehow, not killed or wounded.

He thought for a moment, slowly shrugged off his pack, and settled it on the ground behind him. The others clustered close, under the nets.

"I'm going to distract the guards. When they're gone, just walk across the street and go into the market, carrying my pack. I'll meet you at the . . . biggest pie seller."

"What if there isn't a pie seller?" whispered Conor.

"There's always a pie seller," Rollan said indignantly.

"In Zhong?" asked Abeke. "I don't think they eat pies."

Rollan hadn't thought of that. He was sure they ate something *like* pies.

Tarik nudged him and pointed across the street to a tower standing tall above the market stalls, about half a mile in. Rollan let out a short sigh of relief.

"Right, we'll meet on the shaded side of that tower. I'll find you. Essix will see you for sure."

"It's risky," said Tarik. "But I see no choice. Take care of yourself, Rollan."

"I always do," said Rollan with a confident wink.

He pulled out his knife and cut away a big square of fishing net, winding it around his head like a turban and letting a piece fall across his face. Then he took off his blue sailor's jacket and reversed it, to show the paler underside before putting it back on again inside out.

"Wait till they run after me," he whispered, and walked out from under the nets, straight at the guards. They were talking together and didn't notice him at first, not until the stoat stiffened up and made a hissing noise.

Rollan let out a terrifying scream and staggered across into a stand on the edge of the market that was selling beads and necklaces. Dragging down dozens of necklaces and spilling beads all across the road, he pointed at the stoat and screamed, "It spat poison in my eyes!"

The guards swore and advanced upon him, the stoat leaping ahead. Rollan tipped over a basket of beads in front of them, dove under the stallkeeper's reaching arms, and ran into the depths of the market, still howling.

"Poison! Poison!"

4

SECRET SIGNALS

A{S SOON AS THE GUARDS RAN AFTER ROLLAN, TARIK,} Abeke, and Conor moved, sauntering across the road into the market. Their hearts were pounding and all three felt sure that at any moment someone would shout . . . but no one was watching. Everyone nearby was staring at the trail of destruction left by Rollan and the pursuing guards.

By the time the marketgoers turned back to their business, the three disguised Greencloaks were standing in front of a hot food stall, waiting in line to buy a rice-and-meat mixture served on a green leaf. To Abeke it smelled delicious, much more enticing than the food on the ship.

"Hey, puppeteers!" said the food seller, ladling the spicy mixture onto the laid-out leaves. "Where're you doing your show? My daughter loves the shadow plays."

"An inn outside the East Gate," said Tarik.

"Oh, the Bright Moon," said the food seller. "Best rice wine in Kho Kensit! Another reason to come see your show. There you are. Three bits."

Tarik handed over three small silver coins, carefully chosen to be from Eura, Zhong, and Amaya.

"We've not been here long," he said conversationally as he handed the food to Conor and Abeke. "I was worried by all this talk of the Conquerors and the change of government. But everything seems quiet enough."

"All quiet here," said the food seller, suddenly looking down. "Move along, move along, there's people waiting."

The trio left, joining the moving throngs of people. Abeke glanced back at the food seller and was alarmed to see him staring after her. She hoped he would put selling his wares ahead of alerting the guards to strangers. Something Tarik had said made the man suspicious.

As the sun rose, more and more of the cityfolk came out to make their purchases in the market. The narrow lanes between the stalls became much more crowded, noisier, and dustier.

"I hope Rollan hasn't gotten himself caught," muttered Conor to Abeke as they approached the tower that dominated the center of the market.

"He *has* been a bit distracted since Meilin left," said Abeke. "I mean, I'm sure he won't get caught. Fairly sure . . ."

"We might all get caught," muttered Conor, casting anxious eyes over toward a pair of guards who were trying knives at a nearby stall.

"He said the shadowed side, didn't he?" asked Abeke. She was beginning to get really worried. Where was Rollan?

She was just turning her head to the left when Rollan popped up next to her. He was no longer wearing the fishnet turban and his jacket was the right way out. As Abeke gaped at him, he took his own pack back and slung it over his shoulder.

"Thanks," he said. "You ready to head over to the East Gate?"

"We are," said Tarik. "The guards . . . ?"

"Led them on a wild-goose chase to a cesspit where the marketeers throw their trash. A particularly horrible one, judging by the smell. They, um, tripped, and won't be going anywhere for a while."

"Well done, Rollan."

Rollan puffed up his chest. "Follow me, then," he said.

"We must avoid being overconfident," Tarik warned, before Rollan could dart off again. "Ask Essix to check the way ahead."

"I have."

"She must stay up high. If she's spotted as a spirit animal—"

"Don't worry, she's being careful," said Rollan with a flash of irritation. But he did seem calmer, and that made Abeke feel less nervous in turn. Keeping a low profile was the priority. Stunts like the one Rollan had just performed were dangerous, even if they were clever.

"That was quick thinking back there," she told him as they wandered through the market, pretending to be innocent passers-through. "I guess you had a lot of practice back in Concorba."

Rollan made a rolling gesture with his hand, one way and then the other.

"What does that mean?" asked Abeke.

"Oh, it's a sign the street people use," he said. "It means 'just a bit' or 'not so much.'"

"We have hunting signs," said Abeke. "It isn't possible to speak when the stalkers close on the prey."

"Show me some," said Rollan. "I'll teach you the ones we used in Concorba."

They traded Amayan and Niloan hand signals as they wove through the crowd. Some of the gestures were similar. A quick twist of his left hand meant "pickpocket" to Rollan, but "take cover" to Abeke. Spying guards at one end of a laneway, Abeke pointed with two fingers over her head to an empty stall, and he understood her intentions immediately. She ducked through the stall and out the rear, followed closely by the others.

A stall owner called out angrily to them as they passed. Abeke couldn't understand the words, but she recognized the look of hate in his eyes, and the anxiety of the other nearby marketgoers.

Eventually they left the market quarter and the itchy feeling along Abeke's spine began to ease slightly. They climbed up a zigzag road into a more prosperous quarter, where merchants had their permanent shops. The streets were still busy, so it was easy for the foursome to mingle with the moving crowd. But they still stood out, with clothes that were damp from their early-morning wade and disassembled puppets towering over their heads.

When they neared the East Gate, the foot traffic slowed and began to thin out. They could see the city wall running to the right and left, and the great gatehouse in the middle. A flag was flying above it, showing the blazon of the Conquerors. The great gate beneath was only half open, one of its two leaves shut. Guards stood in the open space, inspecting everyone going in and out, a line of people patiently waiting on either side.

"Remember your names," whispered Tarik. He meant their false names, practiced on the ship. "We're puppeteers going to do a show at the Inn of the Bright Moon, just stick to that."

He stopped talking as the line inched forward. There were half a dozen guards in the gateway, actively inspecting travelers as they passed through. Two of them had spirit animals, one a brutish, heavy-shouldered dog that sniffed every traveler, and the other a massive spider that sat on its partner's shoulder, a thick strand of web hanging from its spinnerets down her arm.

"Names and business!" snapped the guard with the dog spirit animal.

"Mosten," said Tarik. "Shadow puppeteer, going to do a show at the Inn of the Bright Moon. These are my apprentices, Olk, Snan, and Pahan."

The dog sniffed at Tarik, then circled around and sniffed each of the others in turn. But it didn't then sit back on its haunches. Instead it sniffed everyone again, most particularly Abeke. Then it looked up and growled at her.

"Smagish doesn't like you," growled the guard. "You smell funny."

"I just played with a kitten," she said quickly. "I wanted to buy it, but Mosten wouldn't let me. Said we had to spend our silvers on something useful."

"Silvers?" asked the guard. "You got money?"

"Of course," said Tarik. "They wanted five silvers for the kitten, which is robbery."

"Vagrants with no money wandering around is robbery

waiting to happen," said the guard. "Show me."

Tarik held out five silvers in his palm. The guard looked around, then scooped the coins up.

"That's a fine," he said. "For playing with cats and wasting my time. Off you go."

They started forward, but suddenly the woman with the spider spoke.

"Wait," she said.

Rollan tensed, waiting for the spider to jump, or for a sudden attack. But the spider just sat there, and the woman didn't go for her weapons.

"What about me?" she asked. "Where's my share?"

"We've only got three more between us," whined Rollan.

"Hand 'em over!"

Tarik shrugged and made a show of searching his pouch before he reluctantly pulled out some more coins. The woman took them with a disgruntled expression.

"You could give one to her," suggested Rollan to the dog-faced guard. "Then you'd have four each."

"I already got mine," said the first guard.

"Give me one," said the woman.

They started to argue. Rollan moved off, making the hand sign that meant "hurry" to Abeke. But she needed no sign, nor did the others. They all rushed through the gate, leaving the guards bickering behind them.

Past the gate, Abeke was surprised to see dozens of tiny houses built up close to the city wall, which wouldn't be allowed in any of the cities she had seen in Eura. Row after row of narrow doorways opened onto tiny hutches barely large enough for chickens but in which whole families lived. People squabbled and fought over scraps with scrawny dogs that themselves looked more like rats. Continuing along the road, she realized that these areas belonged to the very poor. These roughly made huts with makeshift roofs and walls could be quickly knocked down if the ground in front of the wall needed to be cleared to help defend against an enemy attack. Only they hadn't done it, and now the Conquerors had taken over.

"Ugh," said Abeke, crinkling her nose with distaste at a strong smell of sewage. Such uncleanliness would never have been tolerated in her village. "I wanted to get out of the city, but this is even worse."

"We will be out into the country soon enough," said Tarik quietly. "We just need to meet the messenger and find out where we need to go."

"Is that the inn?" asked Rollan, pointing to a large building that stood head and shoulders above the surrounding shacks. It also had a low wall around it, to keep the surrounding slum at bay. Above the wooden gate there was a hanging sign, showing a bright crescent moon rising from behind a mountain.

"It is," said Tarik, "but we don't want to stay here. I'll seek out the messenger and we'll be on our way as quickly as possible."

They walked under the inn sign and through the gate, and then stopped in their tracks. The courtyard of the inn was full of soldiers. Dozens of them were sitting around on upturned barrels. Even worse, there were dozens of spirit animals as well.

The whole place was an enemy camp!

5

INN OF THE BRIGHT MOON

CONOR HESITATED, AND BEGAN TO TURN AROUND. BUT Tarik took his arm and held him firm.

"Running will only make us look suspicious," he whispered.

Rollan agreed. "Got to pretend we belong here, even though we don't. Keep going!"

Hunching close together, the quartet moved toward the front door of the inn, along the narrow lane between the soldiers. Heads turned as they passed, conversation stopped, and they felt the stares of both humans and animals. A thin snake coiled around the neck of a soldier tasted the air with its flickering tongue, and aimed its unblinking eyes at them, as though sensing something odd about them. Two mismatched weasels stopped fighting to stare. Conor braced himself to release Briggan at the first sign that they had been discovered. Hiding was all very well, but he wasn't afraid to fight if there was no other choice.

Just as Tarik put his foot down on the first of the three steps to the front door, it was flung open. A tall man in a not terribly white apron, with a belt of cups around his waist – indicating he was the innkeeper – appeared in the doorway and threw up his arms in relief.

"Puppeteers!" he cried. "I sent for actors, minstrels, anything! But puppeteers are perfect. How much for a show, and can you start *very soon* now?"

Tarik looked momentarily startled, and Rollan stepped into the breach.

"A dozen silvers and dinner," he said. "But we'll need it to be a bit darker for the show. Say the sixth hour."

"Done!" exclaimed the innkeeper. He looked around at the seated soldiers, who had returned to their card games, drinks, and conversation. "Name's Bowzeng. I've got a troop of fifty Conquerors billeted here, bored as anything and needing distraction, and not from breaking up my furniture, if you please. Come in."

He turned around and clattered back inside. Abeke pulled at Rollan's sleeve.

"Have you gone crazy?" she whispered. "We don't know how to do a show!"

Conor nodded vigorously in agreement. He had helped the ship's carpenter build the puppets, but had never once tried to use them.

"We won't have to," whispered Tarik. "Rollan knows what he's doing. Follow his lead."

Rollan glowed at the senior Greencloak's words, and Conor felt a twinge of jealousy. The puppets were *his* idea. Without them, they'd have been captured already.

Inside the inn, there was a large common room full of even more soldiers. Bowzeng indicated a slightly raised platform down at the far end.

"You can put your screen across the front there," he said. "There's hooks in the ceiling. I will announce the performance . . . ah . . . What is the name of your troupe?"

"Mosten's Most Marvelous Puppets," said Rollan. "We'll set the screen up and get ready, but like I said, it's still too light."

"We can close the shutters," said Bowzeng. He looked around again. The soldiers were sitting and drinking, occasionally bursting into vigorous argument over cards and dice. Many of the soldiers showed the tattoos of the Marked, but the spirit animals were either in dormant form or sticking close to their partners. From the way Bowzeng's eyes darted around, he expected the Conquerors to cut loose any second.

"We need the time to prepare everything," said Rollan easily. He led the way over to the platform and set down his pack, helped Abeke with hers, and took off the rolled-up sail. "You carry on with whatever you need to do, Master Bowzeng."

The innkeeper looked troubled, but bustled away and started calling out to one of his serving people.

"More of everything for our honored guests!" he called out.

"Get the screen up," hissed Rollan to Abeke, but Conor knew he meant him as well. Rollan just wouldn't look him in the eye. "Uh, Mosten, I think we should get some fire buckets to have by the big lantern. Can you help me find some?"

Tarik nodded, and the two of them slipped off into the kitchens.

"Come on, then," said Abeke encouragingly to Conor. He started, and realized he was still thinking about Rollan ignoring him. Woolgathering, which was never helpful. He started to unroll the sail, Abeke cheerfully grabbing the other end and pitching in.

They had just managed to get the sail hung up evenly across the end of the common room, after some trial and error, and set up the big lantern on a stool behind it, when Tarik and Rollan returned. Both were carrying large wooden buckets slopping over with water.

Shielded by the screen from the soldiers, the four gathered around the packs and started to pull out the pieces of the shadow puppets.

"I found the messenger," whispered Tarik. "We worked together a few years ago and he recognized me the moment we went out back. He's working here as a cook. He has good news: One of our finest people, a Greencloak named Lishay, has found Dinesh. We have to meet up with Lishay as soon as possible. The rendezvous is deep in Kho Kensit, quite a distance from here. Fortunately, we can get a good part of the way there by canal and river. The jungles of Kho Kensit are not easy to travel otherwise."

"If we leave the puppets and everything, we'll make better time," said Abeke.

"Agreed," said Conor, who was heartily sick of lugging the heavy screen around. "We can sneak out the back way and be miles away before anyone notices."

"That's my plan exactly," said Rollan with a satisfied smirk. "I told you we wouldn't have to do a show."

They emptied their packs and left the puppets leaning up against a dirty wall. Using the distraction of a particularly bawdy song, which had the entire inn joining in for its chorus, they proceeded in a line with Tarik at the lead through the kitchens and out a small back gate.

They found themselves in an alley that was stacked with empty barrels, broken pots, and other rubbish from the inn.

"See? Easy," said Rollan, still grinning.

"We were lucky," said Tarik in cautionary tones. "I think that innkeeper was right. He will have trouble there tonight."

"Particularly without a puppet show," said Conor. "I feel a bit sorry for him."

"Hey, we have to do whatever's necessary for our mission," said Rollan. "Most of us, anyway."

"What do you mean by that?" asked Conor, bristling.

"Just what I said," said Rollan easily.

"I know what you meant," said Conor.

"Rollan's right," said Abeke, although she cast an apologetic glance at Conor. "Within reason. Beware the lion hunter becoming the lion."

"What does *that* mean?" Rollan asked.

"It's an old saying from my village," she told him. "Some people turn into the thing they're fighting, if they're not careful."

"Who's not being careful? We're safe now, aren't we?"

"Not yet," said Tarik. "There's a barge waiting for us, but the canal is along the street and then down the hill. Without the puppets, we will be dangerously exposed."

Rollan may have lived in a city, but Conor had lived in a

town, and people were the same there. He was determined to show Rollan that not everything he said was stupid.

"Pick up something that could be cargo we're taking to the barge," he said, indicating the rubbish.

He picked up a small barrel himself. Rollan took a rice wine pitcher and Abeke a sack that she turned around to hide the hole in the back. Tarik chose a crate, putting his pack in it before hoisting it up on his shoulder.

They were just setting out when a slurred voice called out from the back gate.

"Where you going? S'posed to do a show!"

It was a soldier. One of the Conquerors. A particularly large soldier, standing in the doorway and scowling.

Rollan, Abeke, and Conor moved as one, without the need for speech.

Conor stepped to the side and swung his barrel in front of the soldier's feet, sending the man tumbling forward. Abeke opened her sack and jammed it over the soldier, muffling his shouts, and Rollan hit his sack-wrapped head with the rice wine pitcher. The man collapsed to the ground, unconscious.

"Well done!" said Tarik.

The three youngsters looked at each other. Rollan grinned at Conor. For a moment Conor felt a kind of weight lifting from his spirit, and he hesitantly began to smile back. Then Rollan seemed to remember himself. He frowned, and Conor too turned the beginnings of his smile into a look of concentration. There was no time for congratulations, anyway. The sound of raised voices was growing louder from inside the inn. Pausing only to pick up a new barrel, sack, and pitcher, they sped off along the alley.

Behind them, the door crashed open.

"Hey!"

"This way," said Tarik, turning left along a lane that was barely larger than the alley. Conor heard something smash behind them, but he didn't turn to see. Heavy footsteps followed them. He had to concentrate on keeping ahead of them.

A whistle sounded, two rising pitches, and suddenly there were Conquerors ahead of them too, at the end of the lane, alerted by their compatriot's signal.

"Through here." Tarik ducked into an entranceway and along a cobbled area full of pigs. The stones were slippery underfoot. "Yah!" said Tarik, slapping one of the pigs on the rump as he passed. "Yah!"

They ducked into another lane and this time Conor did glance over his shoulder. Two Conquerors were hot on their heels. The first tripped over a pig. The second slipped on the cobbles.

Conor grinned and returned his attention forward to where Tarik was hurrying the others along the lane.

The grin was replaced by a gasp of panic as a Conqueror suddenly burst through a doorway immediately to Conor's right, beefy hands clutching for his hair.

"Got you!"

Conor ducked and threw the barrel at his face. The man was between him and Rollan, so without even thinking Conor backpedaled and went the other way up the lane, as fast as his legs could carry him. The Conqueror roared and followed, moving heavily but with frightening speed.

At the end of the lane there was no time for active

thought. His heart racing, Conor turned right, ending up close to the wall again, and there were people everywhere. He ducked and wove between them, but he could hear the Conqueror right behind him, people shouting and screaming as he pushed them aside.

Fear helped him run faster. He could almost feel his pursuer's breath on his neck, and his shoulders tensed with the expectation of a sudden blow, maybe even a knife thrust —

Ahead, two more Conquerors stepped into his path and raised their weapons. Excited spirit animals — a cat and a frill-necked lizard — hissed. Conor couldn't fight them on his own. He had to find some way to escape — but where? There were only walls around him, the thin, narrow walls of Xin Kao Dai's shantytown.

That gave him an idea. These places weren't constructed with solid stone like back home. The walls were literally paper-thin here; he could burst through them if he had to. But as well as paper there were hanging screens made of cloth. He pushed one aside and ran through to the home behind it.

A young man was sitting at a clay pot, stirring something thin and gruel-like over a miserly flame. He looked up in surprise.

"Sorry," gasped Conor, crashing through to the next house along.

Behind him, he heard paper walls tearing.

He paused for a moment to gasp for air, his eyes wide and searching, hoping he would see some new way out.

A small hand gripped his. Conor looked down and saw a young child tugging at him, as though telling him to follow. Behind her, an elderly woman nodded and made an urgent shooing gesture.

The girl pulled his hand harder. The shouting and the wall-destroying noises were too loud and too close.

Conor let the girl lead him away. She took him at a skipping run through a series of cloth and paper tunnels, deeper into the shantytown. People watched him as he passed through, led by the girl along a maze he could never have navigated on his own. None of them interfered.

Slowly, the sound of pursuit fell behind them. Still the girl tugged his hand. He followed her until they reached the edge of the shantytown, where she carefully peeled back a cloth the color of mud. The light seemed bright to Conor's eyes, and he had to blink twice before he understood what he was seeing.

It was the canal. A long barge floated on it, heavily laden with cloth bales, and there, next to it, were his friends. Their faces were set with tension, and Abeke kept glancing up the street, searching for Conor. Rollan looked particularly worried – or was that simply annoyance? Conor couldn't tell.

"Thank you," he told the girl before running to join them. He wished he had some of the silvers Tarik had given the guards at the gate. But she didn't stick around to accept his thanks. With a quick smile, she turned and disappeared into the shadows.

Conor stepped out into the light, waved, and hurried across the exposed thoroughfare to join the others at the side of the barge that would take them into the jungle, toward Dinesh and the Slate Elephant Talisman.

6

XUE

NIGHT CAME, AND THE RATS CAME CREEPING THROUGH the bamboo to eat the fallen flowers. Meilin kicked at them, but in her weakened state they did little more than retreat a foot or so. Her stomach was an aching void, her throat felt as if she had swallowed a thornbush, and her limbs felt both heavy and distant. The rats didn't consider her a threat, even with her quarterstaff. How long, she wondered in weary desperation, until they started considering her *food*?

She had lost track of the days. Once again, she was at an intersection of paths in the Great Bamboo Maze, and there was no indication of which one would lead to freedom, water, or any kind of sustenance. Every strategy she had tried had met with failure.

Jhi butted her hip and sat down heavily, dragging at her with her paw.

Meilin hesitated, then gave in and slowly sat down, almost collapsing into a bed of bamboo flowers. She didn't have the strength to fight her spirit animal anymore.

Jhi raised a paw to her ear and moved her head very slowly from side to side.

"Listen? You want me to listen?" asked Meilin. "To what?" Meilin frowned, but she listened.

At first all she could hear was the faint rustling of the bamboo as some breeze high above moved the topmost shoots. It certainly didn't penetrate down below, where the air remained humid and still.

She heard the rats rustling around her, occasionally squeaking at each other. There were so many of them, growing fat on the fallen flowers while she starved.

Jhi leaned against her, and Meilin felt her anger and frustration diminishing. She felt a calmness descend upon her, and she became aware that she was breathing in the same rhythm as the panda. A sense of peace was flowing into her through the link she had with her spirit animal.

She did not know how long she sat, just listening. When Jhi finally heaved herself up, it was night and there was a rat nibbling the toe of Meilin's left shoe. She swished her quarterstaff at it, and it retreated, rustling in its haste to get away from her.

The Maze was now completely dark, the thick bamboo above hiding even the starlight. Meilin couldn't see anything at all, not even her own hand held up close to her face. She stood up too, holding Jhi's fur just behind the panda's head. Despite the darkness and the rats and the incessant gnawing of her gut, she still felt calm. Panda and girl stood like statues, hardly breathing. Her pulse quickened as she heard a faint noise far away, because it was not a natural sound. It was metallic, the soft clang of metal, like a fork upon a tin plate.

"There's someone nearby," whispered Meilin.

Jhi stirred at her side and began to walk away. Meilin clutched at her fur.

"Where are you going?"

The panda stopped to let Meilin get a better grip, then ambled off again. Meilin followed her in the total darkness, trusting that her spirit animal would find the way.

It was strangely liberating to just follow the panda in the dark. Meilin couldn't see the thick bamboo walls of the Maze. She couldn't see where they were crossing intersections of the paths, and so couldn't feel the terror of not being able to choose the right one.

Meilin shut her eyes and placed all her trust in Jhi. Even the day before, Meilin would probably have shouted at the panda, asked Jhi where she was taking her, if she was taking her anywhere at all. But tonight she didn't. She stayed calm, and kept her eyes shut, and followed.

Jhi changed direction. Meilin's shoulder crashed against some bamboo stalks, but not hard. The descent of night had cooled the air. It was almost peaceful. All Meilin had to do was hold on and walk slowly.

How long they walked toward the faint metal noise she didn't know. They moved very slowly, and every now and then Jhi would stop and reach between the tall bamboo for some smaller plant, pulling it down and breaking it until she got the succulent shoots at the top, every time showering Meilin with flowers and small insects.

The sound grew louder and clearer as they walked, the panda unhesitatingly choosing each turn in the Maze. Meilin wondered what the sound could be. It was very soft and faint, but certainly metallic. She was sure she never would have heard it while she was running around, or even walking, desperately trying different paths.

Then Jhi turned a corner and Meilin saw the faintest glow through her closed eyelids. She opened her eyes, and up ahead she saw the soft light of a campfire. An iron tripod stood above the fire, with a traveling cauldron suspended from it. There was a small, hunched-over figure stirring the pot with a long metal ladle. That was the sound Meilin had heard. Not the harsh ring of a spoon hitting the cauldron, just the soft scrape and ting as the ladle went gently around and around inside the rim.

As Meilin drew closer, she could see the little figure was a silver-haired old woman wrapped in a dark cloak. A very tall pack was propped nearby against the bamboo, a pack loaded with small pots and pans and spoons and knives, a kind of traveling kitchen. The woman was cooking. Meilin couldn't tell what was in the pot, but it smelled absolutely wonderful.

Suddenly all her hunger, forgotten in her long walk with Jhi, returned. It felt like a physical punch to her gut. It was all she could do not to double over and fall piteously to the ground.

"Greetings, Old Mother," croaked Meilin politely. Her voice hardly sounded human, she thought, her throat was so dry. "May . . . a lost traveler ask for some food and water? I have money; I can pay."

The woman turned her head, her sharp black eyes looking Meilin up and down where she stood in the flickering firelight. Then her eyes darted to Jhi.

"Payment?" she said. "No payment is necessary for

aiding the lost. Nor should it be asked. Come, share my fire, my food, my water."

"Thank you," said Meilin. She felt weak in the knees, as much with relief as weariness, as she slowly sank down next to the woman. "My name is Meilin. And this is—"

"Jhi," interrupted the woman. She handed Meilin a small but beautiful porcelain cup and filled it with cool, clear water from a waterskin. "I had heard talk of the return of the Great Beasts. My name is . . . You can call me Xue."

Meilin barely heard her. The water looked magical by firelight—so clear and bright, as if it were a pure crystal catching the reflection of the red and yellow flames—and when she brought the cup to her lips, she had to fight the instinct to gulp. She knew that would make her sick. Instead she sipped at it, taking one small mouthful and slowly allowing it to trickle down her throat. Her body sang with relief. She almost wept. Perhaps the water *was* magical. It tasted better than any palace cordial.

When the cup was empty, Meilin held out her shaking hands for more. Xue refilled it three times, until finally Meilin judged that she had had enough, for now.

"Would you like some of my stew?" asked Xue.

"Yes, please," said Meilin. "It smells good. What is it?"

"Rat and bamboo shoots," said Xue. "There's no other source of meat left in the forest now. Just thousands and thousands of rats, eating the flowers."

"Oh," said Meilin. She hesitated, then said firmly, "I would like some, please, Madam Xue."

"Just Xue," said the old woman. She leaned around and opened her pack, drawing out a beautiful porcelain bowl from a padded pocket, and a matching spoon. She ladled a modest helping into the bowl and passed it to Meilin.

She dipped in her spoon and raised it to her mouth, just as a flower fell from above, right into the stew. Xue reached over and picked it out with a pair of very sharp-pointed chopsticks that had apparently come out of her sleeve, the movement so fast Meilin almost didn't see it.

"The bamboo dies, bedecking its own grave with flowers," said Xue. "It has been a long time since the Maze needed replanting."

"Who will replant it?" Meilin said bitterly. "The Devourer and his Conquerors have crushed Zhong. They have taken the Wall, and now the Maze dies."

"All is not lost," said Xue. "The Devourer's troops are like the skin on a rice pudding, a shallow covering that can easily be torn aside. Besides, there are still those of Zhong who resist."

"You know where there are loyalists? Enemies of the Devourer?" asked Meilin excitedly, her determination undimmed now that she had food in her stomach. "That's who I have come to find! To help! Where are they?"

Xue looked across at Jhi, who was contentedly chewing on bamboo shoots. The panda flicked her ears.

"There is a camp not far away," she said. "There have always been hidden fortresses within the Maze. The loyalists gather at the South Fort."

"The South Fort?" asked Meilin. "But . . . but I was crossing in the north. The Northern Entrance to the Maze."

"Impossible. You could not have gotten here from there. You must have come in the Southwestern Entrance."

Meilin stared at the old woman.

"No wonder I got lost," she said, aghast. "I was following

the instructions for the wrong part of the Maze!"

"You are fortunate that you have the companionship of Jhi," said Xue. "No panda is ever lost in a bamboo forest, even one grown deliberately as a maze."

"Yes," said Meilin. "But I didn't listen to her. Not at first."

"In silence, thought begins," said Xue. "Eat your stew. Sleep. In the morning, I'll guide you to the South Fort."

"Thank you," said Meilin. "I . . . I don't know what I would have done without your help."

"You have Jhi," said Xue, as if she didn't even understand what Meilin was talking about.

"Yes," said Meilin. She turned to the panda, who was pulling down yet another bamboo stalk. "Thank you, Jhi."

Jhi didn't stop shredding bamboo shoots, but Meilin felt a feeling of warmth pass between them, a kind of mental hug. She smiled, lay down next to the panda, and went instantly to sleep.

7

TWO TIGERS

I DON'T LIKE THIS JUNGLE," SAID ROLLAN. "GIVE ME A CITY anytime."

"Really?" asked Abeke in surprise. "I prefer my home, of course. It is not so wet and misty. But it is still better here than in any city. Uraza likes it too."

It was two days since they had escaped Xin Kao Dai. The small party was now sitting in the bow of a slow but comfortable river barge, under a gauzy awning that protected them from the sun, from the teeming insects of the jungle all around the canal, and from prying eyes. Briggan sat next to Conor. The blue-eyed wolf watched the jungle riverbank with suspicion, while Uraza lay sprawled half across Abeke's lap and half across a bale of some kind of spice, one of many piled high on the barge's deck. Essix, of course, was somewhere aloft.

"I'll be happy to get off this boat, though," added Abeke. "I have been too much on boats."

"The *Tellun's Pride* was all right," said Rollan. "A lot

more comfortable than I expected."

"I was on a ship before that," said Abeke. "When I left my home."

"With the enemy . . ." Conor started to say.

"Yes," said Abeke quietly. "Though I didn't know it."

Briggan shifted at Conor's side, his ears pricking up. Uraza lifted her head too, and sniffed the air. Up above, Essix called, a cry that was not her normal hunting whistle.

The three straightened up and looked ahead. The barge was heading for a point where the river narrowed for a stretch, and there were islands of matted reeds, some of them big enough to conceal bandits or river-pirate boats.

Abeke reached for her bow, quickly strung it, and nocked an arrow. Conor picked up his ax, and Rollan drew his knife with one hand and pulled back the gauze curtains with the other.

"I can't see any trouble," said Abeke, scanning the heavily vegetated riverbanks.

Conor walked back between two of the bales stacked on the deck and called down into the cabin.

"Tarik!"

There were two crewmen some sixty feet back at the stern of the barge, but they didn't look alarmed. One was trimming the large, single sail, hauling on the main sheet, while the other held the massive tiller.

Briggan growled and stood stiff-legged, responding to some unseen, scented threat. Uraza jumped up onto the bale right at the bow and stared off toward the jungle bank, her tail twitching.

"What is it?" asked Abeke, sensing the unease of her spirit animal. It felt like all the hairs on her arms and neck were standing on end.

"Essix is definitely picking up something weird," said Rollan. "I don't know what, though."

"Could there be an enemy in those reeds?" asked Conor anxiously. Abeke looked where he was pointing. The barge was going to pass very close to an island of swaying river plants, where attackers could easily be hiding.

"Of course there could be," said Rollan. He kept pulling back the gauze curtains, disturbing the biting insects that had clustered against the gauze.

Suddenly the reeds parted. There was a deafening yowl, the flash of movement – and a huge tiger leaped onto the barge. A black tiger, with charcoal-colored fur marked with midnight stripes.

It landed on the spice bales and lunged down at Abeke's head. She jumped back, dropping her bow. Uraza leaped to her defense, even though the leopard was much smaller than the tiger. They slashed at each other, jumping from bale to bale, with Briggan following on the deck, lunging at the tiger's tail. Essix hovered overhead, wings beating the air furiously, her screech adding to the cacophony.

Rollan and Conor stood on opposite sides of the barge, weapons ready. The combat was so fast and furious that they didn't dare join in. The two big cats moved quickly across the bales, yowling ferociously with every bite and scratch. Most of these failed to connect until Uraza suddenly landed a blow on the tiger's ear, her claws tearing a deep notch.

Abeke cheered the leopard on, but her cheers turned to a sudden gasp as Uraza failed to entirely twist out of the way of a vicious swipe. Five trails of blood sprang up on her flank, the mark of the tiger's claw.

Briggan howled furiously from the deck, unable to join the combat that danced about on top of the bales.

Abeke grabbed her bow, nocked an arrow, and drew it. But even with her quickness, she couldn't get a clear shot. She was joined a moment later by Tarik, who came rampaging out of the cabin, sword in hand.

"It's a spirit animal," he said. "Maddened beyond reason!"

"We have to help Uraza!" Abeke shouted at him. The tiger was much bigger and stronger than the leopard, though Uraza was slightly faster.

The tiger's jaws snapped at Uraza's throat. Only a wild roll saved her.

"A net!" said Conor. "The fishing net. I'll get it!"

He ran down the side of the barge, narrowly avoiding a spice bale that fell off the top of the stack, dislodged by the squalling big cats. The crew had nets with long handles they used to scoop up fish every now and then. If he could get one, it might hold the tiger long enough to tie it up, or kill it if necessary.

But before Conor reached the net, there was another roar from the reeds and a *white* tiger leaped right over the heads of the Greencloaks, straight into the combat.

"No!" shrieked Abeke, thinking that Uraza would have no chance against two huge tigers. She frantically shifted her aim, trying to get a clear shot, before lowering her bow in amazement.

The white tiger had placed itself between Uraza and the black tiger, and was *helping* Uraza. Its paws batted at the black tiger's head, and when the black tiger tried to get past it, the white tiger butted it firmly away, putting all of its considerable mass to the task. It was the black tiger's turn to stagger, and Abeke waited for the white tiger to lunge for its throat.

But the white tiger held back, and only then did she realize that its claws were sheathed and its mouth was closed. Instead of a fighting roar, it made a strange rumbling noise deep in its throat. Not a purr, but not exactly a growl either. Something she couldn't interpret.

Whatever the white tiger was doing, it worked. The black tiger retreated from Uraza, and then with a last throaty scream of defiance or madness, it jumped from the barge back to the reed island, only the tip of its raised tail visible as it raced into the jungle.

"What was that?" asked Rollan, staring wild-eyed.

"That was my brother's spirit animal," said a voice from the rear of the barge. "He has been driven mad with grief."

Abeke spun around, bringing her bow to bear on a woman now standing on the boat, boots dripping from the water. She was tall and slender, dressed in hunting leathers, with a green silk scarf tied around her neck and gray-flecked black hair tied back in a long plait. Her face was dark and weathered, but from age or long years in the open, Abeke couldn't tell. Perhaps both. A short Zhongese bow was on her back, and a curved sword at her side.

The woman raised her arm and cried, "Zhosur!" The white tiger jumped toward her and vanished in midair, to reappear as the tattoo of a leaping tiger on her forearm.

Abeke kept the bow trained carefully on her.

"Lishay!" said Tarik, pushing past Abeke with the biggest smile she had ever seen on him. He hurried over to her and clasped both her hands tightly in his. "It has been too long. What is this about your brother?"

Lishay's eyes hooded in pain. Her hands twisted, gripped his in turn.

"Hanzan is dead," she said. "Killed in a skirmish against the Conquerors ten days ago. You see what it has done to Zhamin. He is mad, and strikes out against any spirit animal, thinking them to be things created by the Bile."

Tarik nodded somberly.

"It is a terrible thing, to lose one's partner," he said. "The madness of grief has taken many in such circumstances, human and spirit animal."

"The Conquerors will pay," said Lishay. "In blood."

"Do not fear," said Tarik in a calming voice, and his words were meant for Abeke and the others too. She lowered her bow, and Conor reassured Briggan with a hand in the furry ruff of his neck.

"We *will* defeat them," Tarik said, stepping away from the woman, "but we will not do so alone. Let me introduce you to my companions, the children who have brought the Great Beasts back into the world."

Some of Lishay's anger ebbed as introductions were quickly made, but Abeke could see where Lishay's fingernails had left red welts in Tarik's hands.

"Only three," Lishay said with a frown. "Where are the Zhongese noble girl and Jhi? They would be of great help here. Though Kho Kensit is only an outlying region of Zhong, the people revere Jhi. They would flock to our banners if we could show them the Great Panda."

"Meilin went ahead of us, seeking a way to help the resistance more centrally in Zhong," said Tarik. Conor looked at him with questioning eyes. This was the truth, Abeke supposed, but it certainly wasn't the *whole* truth. "We don't know where she is exactly, right now. My guess is that she will try to cross the Wall."

"She'll do it," said Rollan. "She can really move and fight, that girl."

"We hope she will do it," said Conor. "I'm sorry, Lishay. It was my fault she left. If I hadn't given away—"

"Enough," said Abeke. Everyone who mattered knew what Conor had done and understood why he had done it. They needed to get past it, somehow. "We're not here because of that, and neither is Lishay. Concentrate on getting the Slate Elephant. That's what matters."

"Yes," mumbled Conor. "You're right. I'm sorry."

"Stop being sorry!" she exclaimed, her usual calm breaking out of frustration. "We forgave you already, right, Rollan? Please stop apologizing!"

Conor opened his mouth to say something, probably sorry again, then shut it and nodded firmly.

Lishay was watching them closely, but she too said nothing. Abeke decided in that moment she liked the woman, for keeping silent when no more needed to be said.

"Abeke is correct," Tarik said. "Reaching Dinesh and obtaining the Slate Elephant Talisman is our task. We must set our minds to it. Lishay—your message said you had located the elephant himself? What is our path?"

"It's a bit complicated," admitted Lishay. "I will explain things on the way. We'll leave the river at dusk. There is a good landing spot a few miles ahead, so we will not have to risk wading, and attack from the snakeheads."

"Snakeheads?"

"You've been warned not to trail your hands over the side? Not to go in the water?" asked Lishay. "It is because of the snakeheads. They are fish, as long as my arm, and with many sharp teeth."

"They can't jump, can they?" Conor asked.

"Fortunately not," said Lishay. "We must prepare. What supplies did you bring?"

Rollan didn't move.

"Tell us where we're going, first," he said. "What's complicated?"

Abeke suddenly realized that Lishay had told them about the snakeheads to avoid answering what lay ahead. The Greencloak was holding something back, and Rollan, as per usual, had sensed her deception.

Lishay conceded.

"I am fairly certain that Dinesh is in Pharsit Nang, a small area within the lands of the Tergesh."

"Who or what are the Tergesh?" asked Abeke.

"I've heard of them," said Tarik. "They are a strange people, and very dangerous."

"Will they allow us to search for Dinesh in their lands?" asked Conor.

"They move around a lot," said Lishay. "If we're lucky, we will be able to avoid them."

"And if not?" asked Abeke.

"We will ask politely and hope for the best," said Lishay.

It sounded like a joke, but she wasn't smiling.

"I don't understand," said Rollan.

"The Tergesh is what they call themselves," said Tarik in a grim voice. "To everyone else they are known as the rhino riders."

8

THE JUNGLE PATH

LISHAY PROMISED THEM THAT THE JOURNEY FROM THE river barge through the jungle would not be easy, and she was right. They traveled single file along a narrow trail through dense, wet undergrowth with overhanging trees and dangling vines that dropped leeches on everyone. Even when Essix spied a wider path nearby, Lishay would not let them move off the narrow trail she had chosen.

"The Tergesh ride the wider ways," she said. "We are safer here."

"I don't get it," said Rollan, pushing a broad, wet leaf away from his face. "Their spirit animals are rhinos?"

"No," Lishay explained. "They do not bond with spirit animals, with or without Nectar. No one knows why. Possibly it is because as soon as they can stay on one, every Tergesh child is brought up with a rhino calf, living with it, training with it. . . ."

"Ouch!" Rollan said. "Sounds uncomfortable! But still, a rhino would be too big even for the path Essix can see.

I saw one once, in a traveling fair, and it was huge."

"Rhinos are big," confirmed Abeke. "I have only ever seen them in the grasslands. Never in country as crowded with trees and vines as this."

"The rhinos of Pharsit Nang are not the same as the Niloan rhino," explained Lishay. "They are smaller, faster, and meaner, and they are extremely difficult to tame. Think about that. You have all seen wild horses, yes? Imagine a wild rhino, and what kind of rider it takes to master one. That is why we must avoid them by sticking to the narrow trails."

"I'd be happier if we could avoid these biting insects!" complained Rollan, slapping his cheek. He looked at his hand, on which the crushed insect was smeared into a patch of his own blood. He hated the jungle. He even felt a bit sick, as if he might be coming down with something.

"There are fewer of the blood drinkers in the jungle, away from the river," said Lishay. "But more leeches, and spiders, and stinging ants. Look in your boots each morning, and hang a hammock to sleep in."

"I don't know why they like me so much," complained Rollan, slapping another one. "Go and bite Conor!"

"Your blood must taste better," said Conor.

For once Rollan couldn't think of something snappy in response, and it wasn't just that he was surprised that Conor was finally snarking back. He felt his face where the insects had stung him. Was it his imagination, or was his cheek swelling up a bit?

"We will be able to go faster on a wider road," said Abeke.

"It's still too risky," repeated Lishay. She paused to

slash away some kind of creeper that had grown across the path.

"We've got Essix," said Rollan. "She can see any rhinos coming along the path, and we can take cover."

Essix and Zhosur were the only spirit animals currently out and about. All the others were in dormant form. Even Briggan, who was normally at his happiest in the wild, seemed suspicious of the jungle, perhaps because it was closed in and wet. And though Zhosur had seemed perfectly fine with Uraza, Abeke thought it might be wise to keep the leopard away from the tiger. Tarik's Lumeo was also not keen on the jungle, or was possibly just lazy and wanted to ride. Otters could be like that.

"That's true," said Tarik. "Lishay, time is short. . . ."

"I think the risk is too high," Linshay said. "But if you agree, I will bow to you and take the broader path."

Everyone turned to Tarik, whose forehead was deeply wrinkled in thought.

"Very well, then," said Tarik. "Let us take the easier, faster way. Rollan and Essix can watch for approaching rhino riders. We *must* get to Dinesh before the Conquerors."

"How could they know where Dinesh is?" asked Lishay. "We've been searching for months, and only put all the clues together in these past three days."

"The Conquerors also have a seer," said Tarik. "Like Lenori. And their forces are moving deeper and deeper into Kho Kensit. And also . . . I'm becoming paranoid in my age. War has a way of playing on our anxieties."

Lishay nodded. "Very well. We shall take the wider path."

Zhosur made a low rumbling sound and headed off

through the jungle, breaking from the path. Lishay followed, the others close behind. As they left the path, it started to rain again. It was warm rain, but still annoying. It trickled down under their sailor's coats, and got in their eyes, and just made everything more miserable.

"It's so hot," said Conor. "Hotter even than midsummer, back home. No good for sheep."

"No good for anyone except biting insects," said Rollan, slipping on some wet undergrowth and steadying himself by putting his hand out against a tree trunk.

"Are you all right?"

"I slipped," said Rollan irritably, shrugging Conor's hand off his elbow. "The heat's getting to me too. I'm just not cut out for jungles."

Their hike became easier once they got onto the wider trail. It was about eight feet wide, the undergrowth had been well trampled, and there were no annoying vines hanging down from the trees that clustered on either side, and so no sudden showers of leeches either. The rain also stopped and the sun came out, raising wafts of steam everywhere from the drying vegetation.

"This is better," said Abeke.

"It sure is," said Conor.

Rollan didn't say anything. He felt very tired, and could only nod his head in agreement. There was something he felt he should be doing, but he couldn't remember what it was. Something to do with Essix, who was flying around somewhere.

"Zhosur says there is a clearing up ahead," said Lishay.

"Elephant grass, so no cover. We must cross it quickly. Come on."

She led the way again, at the practiced lope of a hunter, faster than a walk, with Zhosur ambling at her side. Abeke matched her stride, Conor behind her, less graceful but keeping up without difficulty. Rollan came behind, stumbling a little. Tarik brought up the rear, turning often to look behind. Lumeo had emerged from passive form and was now draped over Tarik's shoulder, the otter watching as carefully as the man.

"I think someone's following us," said Tarik quietly to the otter. "We had best keep a careful eye out."

Rollan looked behind him and almost slipped again. The air was misty, or was it something in his eyes? He could see nothing but crushed green foliage on the path behind them, and trees crowding in on all sides.

The clearing they reached was as large as Concorba's Central Market Square back home. Saplings and ferns grew in around the edges, like eager children watching from the outskirts of a game. But the rest of it was the spiky elephant grass Lishay had mentioned. Most of it was waist-high, but some bigger clumps were taller even than Tarik. It didn't look much like real grass to Rollan. It grew too high and had blades like long swords.

Lishay stopped where the jungle began to thin out and looked ahead. Zhosur prowled around, sniffing at the ground, his tail quivering.

"He smells rhinos," said Lishay quietly. "But it may not be recent. What does Essix see, Rollan?"

"Uh, what?" asked Rollan. He tried to concentrate, but he just felt . . . foggy. He couldn't think clearly.

"Where's Essix, Rollan?" asked Abeke. "What can she see?"

Rollan looked up at the sky. He couldn't feel Essix anywhere nearby, and her sense-impressions were vague.

"I'm not sure," he muttered. He wiped his sweaty forehead and blinked. The taste of bird flesh and the crunch of tiny bones filled his mouth. "I think she's eating. But if there was anything, she'd warn us, I'm sure of it."

"Our path continues over there," said Lishay, pointing to the far side of the clearing. "Between those two great trees. But two other trails come in, one on each side. Keep a careful lookout. We must cross as quickly as we can, all together at a run. Is everyone ready?"

The group all nodded. No one noticed that Rollan's nod continued almost to his chest. He jerked back as his chin hit his neck, and wiped more sweat off his forehead. Surely he couldn't be as tired as he felt, he thought. It was just the heat, and once he got out in the clearing there would be more air.

"Zhosur will lead," said Lishay. "Let's go!"

The tiger bounded out into the clearing, with Lishay and Abeke right behind him. Conor was next, with Rollan close behind. Tarik once again came last, staying a good distance behind the others, acting as rear guard.

They were halfway across when Zhosur stopped and roared. It was not like the lion's roar that Abeke had described, but rather a series of connected, throaty snarls. With the tiger's roar, there was sudden movement in the tall tufts of grass all around them.

Small rhinos stood up from where they had been lying in the long grass, hidden from sight. Their riders, short but wiry men and women, leaped onto the rhinos' backs, riding without saddles or reins. They wore cotton robes that crossed across their chest, leaving their forearms and feet free. All of them had long knives at their belts, and either a lance or a long bamboo blowpipe.

The rhinos themselves were as Lishay had described them. Smaller than the Niloan variety, with sharper horns and smart, vibrant black eyes.

There were rhino riders everywhere, at least sixty of them, too many to fight. Escape was the only option. But they were surrounded!

Tarik was the first to move. He was the closest to the riders, and he had Lumeo to help him. He twisted on the spot, ran at the rider behind him, threw Lumeo in the air, and slid under the startled rhino's legs as it thrust its horn up in an attempt to gore the flying otter. Emerging out the other side, Tarik caught Lumeo and slapped the rhino hard on the rump, surprising it so much it staggered away.

"Follow me!" he called to the others. "Hurry!"

The others responded as quickly as they could. Conor called Briggan, and Uraza sprang snarling from Abeke's arm, but the rhino riders were advancing, blowpipes at their mouths. Dozens of tiny darts flew across the clearing. Aided by their spirit animals, the Greencloaks danced, and jumped, and ducked through the storm of darts, trying to keep together, to break past the ever-shifting rhinos and reach Tarik, where he stood just outside the circle, unable to help them.

But Rollan wasn't running with them. He felt really sick now, unable to work out what was going on. One of the small darts struck him on the cheek, just like the biting insects that loved him so much. Rollan pulled it out and looked at it, wondering why they bothered to shoot such tiny, ineffective darts. The point of it was smeared with a dark, sticky material. Rollan stared at it, but he didn't figure out what it was until he heard Lishay shouting, as if from far away.

"Poison! Ware poison on the darts! Don't let them strike your skin!"

But the air was thick with them. Not even Lishay could avoid them. The last thing Rollan saw as the strength rushed out of his limbs and he fell to the ground was Tarik sprinting toward the jungle, much faster than any normal man could run, with several rhino riders crashing after him.

9

UNEXPECTED REUNION

"Ｈow do you know your way through the Maze?" Meilin asked Xue as the old woman unhesitatingly chose to go left at the next intersection of paths. Her pack was so tall that from behind she looked like a mass of pots and pans with legs, but each bit of metal was carefully tied and separated, so that they made hardly any noise.

"Practice," replied Xue shortly.

"When will we get to the South Fort?" asked Meilin.

"Later," said Xue.

Meilin opened her mouth to ask for a more detailed response, then shut it. She had already learned that if Xue didn't want to talk, she wouldn't. The girl stopped to look behind her, to make sure Jhi was keeping up and hadn't stopped to eat bamboo shoots. The panda was about thirty yards behind but at least she was ambling along. A few rats ran across in front of her, some of the many that thronged among the bamboo, eating the fallen flowers.

From somewhere ahead came the sound of axes on bamboo.

Meilin whirled around. Xue had stopped. She was standing completely still, listening.

More axes joined, the single chopping boom multiplying. There were many axes at work, not too far away, accompanied by the sound of bamboo falling.

"Someone's cutting the bamboo," said Meilin, instantly thinking of the Conquerors.

"We will go see," Xue said. "If we are separated, Jhi knows the way to the South Fort."

"Jhi knows the way?" asked Meilin.

"I told her while you slept." Xue shrugged off her huge pack and carefully slid it into the bamboo so that it was hidden from sight. Once again Meilin was impressed with how easily she moved for such an old lady. "Be quiet now. We must sneak up and look."

"It can't be the loyalists you spoke of," said Meilin quietly as they walked toward the noise, thinking of her father. "Only servants of the Devourer would attack the Maze."

Xue nodded and held her finger against her lips for silence. The sound of the chopping was getting much louder, loud enough to drown out any noise they might make, thought Meilin, but she obeyed anyway. She looked around again, and was surprised to see Jhi had caught up with them and was only a few steps behind. She didn't know the panda could move so quickly.

They all stopped a few yards short of the next intersection. The sound of chopping was really loud, interspersed with occasional shouts and orders. There had to be hundreds of people at work, and they were close. Xue and Meilin crept forward slowly.

The path only went for a dozen yards or so before it opened out into a great highway that was being cut through the Maze. There was a line of ax wielders stretching far into the distance, all busily chopping away. Other workers were dragging the fallen bamboo back to huge piles that were probably going to be burned.

Behind the line of workers, there were soldiers, many of them with spirit animals. Like the attackers at Jano Rion, they did not wear uniforms, but Meilin had no doubt who they were. They carried whips as well as their weapons, and used them whenever the workers slowed down.

"If you cannot think through something, you destroy it," said Xue. "That is the way of the Devourer. We must—"

She stopped in mid-sentence. The supersharp chopsticks Meilin had seen the night before suddenly appeared in the old woman's hands, and she lunged up into the air above Meilin's shoulder. There was a scream, and a hooded, masked figure dressed entirely in the yellow-green of the bamboo fell to the ground.

Meilin whirled around, her staff raised just in time to counter a vicious strike from the dagger of another camouflaged attacker. She knocked the weapon aside and followed it up with a blow to the collarbone that made the assassin drop the dagger and howl in pain, her arm hanging limp and useless.

But more assassins were jumping down to the path. Meilin backed up, her eyes flickering across them and up into the bamboo, noting the iron spikes driven into the stalks. These enemies had been lurking up there, standing on the spikes, ready to jump down on anyone passing underneath. A series of piercing whistles echoed through the bamboo forest, raising the alarm.

"We must go," said Xue, pointing with her blood-stained chopstick to the right-hand path. Two assassins had dropped there, and there were more above. "Now!"

She charged forward, Meilin at her side. There was a blur of chopsticks and staff, and the two blocking assassins fell wounded to either side. Their companions above were too slow, dropping behind the old woman and the girl.

But Jhi had been left behind, and now there were half a dozen assassins between Meilin and the panda.

"Jhi!" shouted Meilin, raising her arm. She might be too far away, but if Jhi could assume the dormant state, then they could flee. There was a chance. . . .

Jhi didn't return to her. Instead the panda calmly reached up and uprooted one of the shorter bamboo stalks, grunting as she lifted the massive thirty-foot-long stalk completely out of the ground. Gripping it clumsily between her paws, she let it fall straight down the path, toward the heads of the assassins. They jumped aside, the huge length of bamboo bouncing off the ground.

Jhi did not let go. She shook the bamboo, sweeping the path from side to side, catching the assassins' legs and sending them toppling. When the last of them was groaning on the ground, the panda dropped the bamboo and sauntered along toward Meilin, who was staring open-mouthed at her companion.

But she did not have much time to marvel. The guards from the clearing operation had heard the whistled alarms, and a score or more were running toward them with spirit animals outpacing them in front. Meilin noticed one in particular, an ibex with large backswept horns. She was sure she had seen it at the fall of Jano Rion.

"We must run," said Xue.

"We need to slow them down," said Meilin. She looked at Jhi, new admiration for the panda filling her mind.

"Jhi, can you block the path? With bamboo?"

Jhi responded by pulling down a long bamboo stalk across the path, and then another, and then a third, weaving it through the first two in a display of both great strength and precision. In just a few minutes, she added half a dozen more, blocking the path completely.

"Now we run," said Meilin. Jhi made a kind of bleating noise.

"Lazy," said Xue.

Meilin looked puzzled, then laughed and raised her arm. Jhi disappeared, and the panda tattoo appeared on Meilin's hand.

They ran for a surprisingly long time, Xue choosing the turnings with total confidence. Eventually, the sounds of pursuit and cracking bamboo were left far behind them. After a while, Meilin started to hope that Xue would stop for a rest, because she was out of breath herself. Surely an old woman couldn't run so far?

Finally Xue slowed and began to walk.

"Soon you'll come to the South Fort, a left and a right and then straight ahead," she said. "I will leave you now."

"Leave me?" asked Meilin, surprised. "Where will you go?"

"Back for my pack," said Xue.

"Back? But the enemy is there!"

"I will go around them," said Xue, as if this was as easy in the Maze as anywhere.

"Oh," said Meilin. "I was hoping you might . . . might come with me. With us. I've seen you fight. I know I could learn from you, and you could help the loyalists against the Conquerors."

"I have my own business," said Xue. "You fight well too, considering. With practice, one day you might be worth teaching."

Meilin blinked. She was used to being told she was a great student, the best fighter of her age. But she bit back a hurt retort. There was something about the old woman that demanded respect, beyond her fighting ability with sharpened chopsticks, her astonishing endurance and nimbleness. . . .

Suddenly Meilin added two and two.

"Are you one of the Marked?" she asked.

Xue smiled, showing several missing teeth. She opened the top of her silk blouse to reveal a secret pocket. A white jumping mouse blinked up at Meilin, its eyes miniature versions of the old woman's, dark and penetrating and mischievous.

"Zap," she said. The mouse vanished, even as Xue rolled up her sleeve to show the tattoo of a leaping mouse on her forearm.

"Good fortune, Meilin and Jhi. Perhaps we will meet again one day."

Meilin bowed her head. When she looked up, Xue was gone.

The South Fort was half a mile farther along the path, past several intersections. Though still inside the Maze, it was built in a small, shallow valley where many paths met. Meilin came out of the shadow of the bamboo and looked out across the open expanse of bare earth, down to the cluster of huts behind a wooden palisade below. Though there was bamboo forest all around the valley, she still felt cheered to be out of the Maze, at least for now.

"Halt!"

Three soldiers in the crimson-lacquered armor of the regular Zhongese army hurried up toward her. One of them wore the braided armband of a corporal.

"I am Meilin, daughter of–" Meilin started to say, but her words were drowned out by the sudden bark of the corporal.

"Drop your staff and kneel!"

"I will not!" said Meilin. "Escort me to whoever is in command here."

The corporal scowled and drew his sword. A moment later the other two drew their swords as well.

"Our orders are to kill anyone who comes out of the Maze who is not in uniform," he said. "So we will kill you."

"Don't be stupid!" said Meilin, though as she looked at the man's piggish eyes she realized he probably *was* extremely stupid. "Call an officer at once!"

"No peasant out of the bamboo tells me what to do!" roared the corporal. "Kneel down!"

"Corporal, maybe we'd better–" said one of the soldiers, who looked considerably smarter than his superior.

"Shut up!" roared the corporal. He raised his sword. "Intruder, kneel for execution."

"It really would be best to call your officer," sighed Meilin. She raised her own staff. The moves she needed to knock down the three soldiers were already flitting through her head. She knew exactly what to do.

But she didn't attack. Even a few days before, she would have angrily knocked them down and stormed over to the fort to complain to whoever was in charge. But now she kept her anger in check and stood there patiently, just as she had waited patiently with Jhi as night fell in the Maze, for the sound of Xue cooking dinner to become apparent to her. Sometimes patience was the best strategy.

The corporal didn't keep his anger in check. He rushed at her, slashing with his sword. Meilin swayed aside and just slid her staff between his legs so that he stumbled past her and fell over, dropping his sword. He crawled after it, shouting at the others.

"Attack! What are you waiting for?"

The two soldiers looked at each other.

"Attack!" croaked the corporal, from the ground.

The smart-looking soldier sheathed his sword and took a horn from his belt. He blew two sharp blasts from it, the sound echoing across the small valley. A few seconds later, there was an answering pair of blasts from the fort below.

"A patrol will come now," he said. "With an officer. What did you say your name was?"

"Meilin, daughter of General Teng."

The two soldiers exchanged a horrified look, and the corporal on the ground groaned.

"Who is in charge here?" asked Meilin.

The soldiers braced to attention. The corporal staggered up, but only in order to bow low before her.

"The exalted general," blurted the clever soldier.

"General *who*?" she asked, telling herself not to hope.

"Teng, of course. Your father."

Relief ripped through Meilin. He had escaped from Jano Rion after all! He was alive! "Take me to him — immediately!"

"You're really his—" stammered the corporal. "That is, you are really—"

"This way, mistress," said the clever soldier as the patrol appeared, jogging toward them. Once again he had shown he was much quicker on the uptake than his superior. "We will be honored to provide you with a personal escort."

Meilin followed him, feeling a warm rush of happiness. Everything would be all right now that she knew her father was alive. They would soon be together again, and side by side they would fight to wrest Zhong from the clutches of the Conquerors.

With the realization of who she was, everything moved quickly, but not quickly enough for Meilin, who had waited long, hard days for this moment. The loyalist soldiers escorted her into the fort, and she was saluted at the gate to the palisade. Her father was standing on the parade ground, tall in his silver-and-crimson armor, and her eyes pricked with tears on seeing him. It was all she could do not to run to him and throw herself into his arms. But such an open display of affection would shame him in front of his officers. He was standing with several high-ranking loyalists that Meilin knew. He looked tired, she thought, and somehow not quite as tall as she remembered. His uniform was torn, its brilliant insignia gone.

From a distance, she might not have recognized him at all.

"Exalted General," said the soldier, falling back out of respect.

Teng turned and caught sight of Meilin, and his eyes widened in shock.

"Meilin!"

"Father."

She stopped three paces from him and bowed low before him.

His footsteps approached. Two muddy boots came into view. Strong hands gripped her shoulders and raised her to an upright position.

Their brown eyes locked, and in them she saw love and worry in equal measures. And . . . were those *tears* she saw on the brink of falling? Impossible!

For a giddying moment, she thought that *he* might actually embrace *her*.

Then he stepped back, letting her go and allowing his hands to fall to his sides.

"So, you are here," he said. "Why? Are you alone?"

There was a slight tone of rebuke in his voice, which she thought she must surely be misinterpreting.

"I left the Greencloaks, Father, to come back to fight for Zhong," she said. "You should know that a large force of Conquerors is cutting a way through the Maze."

General Teng nodded slowly.

"Your spirit animal, Jhi, is still with you?"

Meilin showed the tattoo on her arm.

"You have learned to work with her, use her powers?"

"I am beginning to learn, Father."

"Good," said General Teng. "We will take tea, and I will hear of your activities. There are . . . things I must tell you too."

"But the Conquerors, Father." She couldn't read him. Why wasn't he worried about the nearness of the enemy? "They are several miles distant, but there is a great host. Hundreds of soldiers at least, forcing many more workers to cut the bamboo."

"It will take them at least a week to cut even a mile through the Maze. General Chin . . . ?"

Her father's closest aide and friend stepped up beside them and nodded at Meilin in recognition. Chin's uniform was worn and didn't appear to have been washed for days. Meilin was relieved to see that he had survived the invasion as well, but if he was relieved to see her in return, he didn't show it.

"Shall I give the order to move out, sir?" he asked General Teng.

"Not yet, but begin preparations, and double the guards on the upper paths," ordered her father. "Is there any chance you were followed through the Maze, Meilin?"

"I'm certain I was not," she said. "We had to fight camouflaged assassins near the cutting, but we got away."

"We?" asked General Teng.

"A woman named Xue helped me," said Meilin. "One of the Marked. I think she used to be a Greencloak. Maybe long ago. She's old, but still strong."

"We know Xue," said General Teng. "She is true to Zhong and a friend of our cause. I'm pleased that she helped you, although somewhat surprised. Come, let's drink tea and we will talk."

"What is there to talk about, Father?" she said. "I've come to fight with you, in your army. Tell me what to do and I will do it."

"Meilin, it is not so simple —"

"It is *perfectly* simple."

"Meilin, enough! Remember who you are."

The rebuke was as startling as a slap. Meilin felt her cheeks grow warm. She knew exactly who she was and what she had traveled so far to do. If he was going to tell her that she was too precious and noble to fight with him against the Conquerors, then he would *really* have a fight on his hands.

Before she could say anything, horn blasts came from higher up the valley, near where Meilin had emerged from the Maze. Four sharp blasts in a row. She knew that signal. It was an alarm, not a call for a patrol.

General Chin let out a gasp of surprise.

"We've been discovered!" snapped General Teng. "To arms, all warriors!"

Gongs took up the alarm, their deep warning chimes echoing through the treetops. Soldiers ran out from the barracks buildings, forming up in ranks.

Teng turned to General Chin. "Take Meilin to the eastern entrance and instruct her on how to reach Pharsit Nang. We'll hold here for as long as possible, then rendezvous with you at the Southeast Supply Camp. Make certain my daughter does not turn back when she leaves you."

"Father, I won't go! Not again!" exclaimed Meilin. "I am a warrior, and I will fight! For Zhong!"

General Teng shook his head firmly.

"You *are* a warrior, yes, but you are a Greencloak too. That is where your duty lies."

"No, Father, it lies with you."

A second time he gripped her by the shoulders, forcing her to look at him. "*No*, Meilin. We have received word that there are Greencloaks in Pharsit Nang. You must find them and rejoin them. You should never have left them. Chin will tell you how to get there. Go now!"

Meilin stared at him, unwilling to accept what he was saying, not caring if he or anyone else saw her tears. How could he send her off again just like that? She didn't want to rejoin the Greencloaks. She didn't believe they could properly resist the Conquerors. Only Zhong, the true Zhong, had the strength to do that.

"Father, I came all this way—"

"Do not argue with me! The Four Fallen are meant to be together, I am sure of this. My hope lies with you, with *them*." He lowered his voice. "And you are not safe among us."

"What . . . what do you mean?"

"The enemy has found us too swiftly for it to be an accident." General Teng was almost whispering now, making sure she and she alone heard him over the sound of soldiers preparing for battle. "There is treachery here . . . or something more sinister. Either way, they want you and Jhi, and I will not let them have you. You will obey me, Meilin. Go now, and go swiftly!"

Meilin stepped away from him, shocked to the core by everything he had told her. Treachery! Among the loyalists! She could barely credit it. But she had to believe him, and she had to accept that what he asked her to do he did in good faith, not because he thought her weak. . . .

"Meilin, you still stand before me! I beg you to go! How can you *still* not see what must be done?"

His words were so harsh, his disbelief so strong. Meilin felt suddenly cold, despite the heat, as if she had been drenched with ice-cold water.

Maybe Jhi *was* meant to be with Essix, Briggan, and Uraza, and that meant Meilin was too. She had left the others in anger—just as Finn had warned her not to before their journey to Eura—a blind anger that had sent her off to seek what she wanted, not what was best. . . .

She blinked back tears. To find her father, and then to be sent away from him again . . . There was a pain in her heart that felt agonizing, but she had to bear it. He was *beseeching* her, not just ordering her. It was as though he was treating her as an equal, an obstinate equal who could not be made to understand something fundamental.

"Yes, Father," she whispered. "I will go at once."

"As you should," he said in a tone she was more familiar with. When she straightened, she thought she caught a hint of a smile behind his stern expression. A sad smile, but it was there.

"General Chin, I'm ready," she said, half turning to address the words to her father's old friend. "Farewell, Father."

"Farewell, Meilin."

They turned away from each other at the same time. General Teng moved quickly to join the soldiers, who were already marching out through the fort's gates. Meilin was hustled in the opposite direction by General Chin, who kept looking over his shoulder, back up the valley.

Meilin looked too, feeling as though a large part of her heart was being left behind with every step.

The battle had already begun. A small group of loyalist soldiers stood shield to shield in the narrow exit from the Maze. But for every enemy they slew, another three hurled themselves against the shield wall, and there were bowmen climbing the bamboo with iron spikes like the assassins who had attempted to waylay Meilin. Within minutes they would be in position, ready to rain arrows down upon the defenders.

Only the narrowness of the path and the bravery of the loyalist soldiers were holding the invaders back. Meilin could hear the shouts and screams and the clash of steel on steel drifting down on the wind. But the defenders could not last, even with her father and his soldiers racing to reinforce them.

"If we're lucky, they will hold till nightfall and can escape under the cover of darkness," said Chin. "I just don't understand how the Conquerors found the way through the Maze so quickly!"

"They didn't follow me," said Meilin defensively. "I'm sure of it! Maybe they've got bird spirit animals, like Essix, and they mapped the Maze from above."

"We shoot all birds," said Chin, and then shook his head, as though dismissing a troublesome thought. "Come. It's two days' hard walking to Pharsit Nang. We must get you away quickly so I can join the fight. I will tell you the turns through the Maze. Listen carefully!"

10

SUNSET DEATH

ABEKE WOKE UP WITH A POUNDING HEADACHE. SHE WAS thirsty and her belly was empty. The sun glared down at her through a gap in clouds that looked fat and heavy, likely to dump a load of rain at any time. She was on her side in very tall grass, unable to move her arms and legs. For a long moment, she couldn't remember what happened. Her limbs appeared to be tied. But how . . . ? Why . . . ?

When she remembered, she groaned more out of dismay than actual pain. There had been too many darts. Even aided by their spirit animals, the Greencloaks could not avoid all of them. Eventually, the darts found unprotected skin, and the poison wound its way into their blood.

Rollan had gone down first, then Conor, both boys dropping heavily onto their backs, limbs splayed. Lishay had rushed to stand with Abeke, but she had been cut down mid-step. First her eyes had rolled back into her skull, then her legs had folded underneath her, and finally she had fallen face-forward to the ground.

Abeke had still worn the Granite Ram, and she used it to attempt a wild leap away. But even as she had passed over the wall of rhinos, a dart had hit the side of her neck. Uraza had yowled somewhere behind her. The world had contracted around her, fading into darkness first at the edges of her vision, then closing in around her, as though she was seeing through a long black tunnel. With the last of her strength she called the leopard back into her tattoo. Uraza could not be harmed there, and might be able to help her when she woke up.

If she woke up . . .

Blinking up at the sky an unknown time later, she told herself to be grateful she was alive, even if she didn't know what she was going to do now. Her hands were tied with a leather cord. The bindings hobbling her ankles had the roughness of rope.

She rolled over and found that Conor and Lishay were lying next to her. Both were awake, and both tied like her. Beyond Lishay, Rollan was lying flat on his back. He was not tied up, but he wasn't moving. He looked very pale, very sick, or even possibly . . .

"Rollan!"

"He's alive," said Conor in response to her gasp. "But he must be very sick. I'm worried about him."

"He was looking a bit ill before," said Lishay. "Or perhaps he has suffered a reaction to the poison."

"We have to help him," Abeke said, sitting up and inching awkwardly across the ground to try to get closer to him. "Any sign of Tarik?"

"None at all," said Conor.

"We won't see him," said Lishay softly, "until he wants

to be seen."

Abeke looked around. The elephant grass was too tall to make out anything of their surroundings, apart from the tops of the usual jungle trees, some distance away.

"Is this the same clearing?"

"No," said Lishay. "We've been moved. We must have been carried here."

"What if they trade us to the Conquerors for some kind of advantage?" Abeke said.

"That is not the riders' way," said Lishay gloomily. "We must face whatever justice they choose to mete out. There's usually a task or trial that we must complete, a very difficult one, in order to prove our innocence. If we can't, they will kill us. Somehow we must prevail."

"But we haven't done anything wrong," said Conor.

"If they were going to kill us," said Abeke, "they would have done it already."

"It's hard to tell," said Lishay. "I think we have been unconscious for two nights."

Abeke shook her head in shock. Two nights! No wonder she felt so parched . . .

"Bring the prisoners!"

The shout startled the Greencloaks. It was followed by the tramp of feet as half a dozen rhino riders came through the grass. Three of them helped Lishay, Abeke, and Conor up, not very gently. The other three picked up Rollan, who hung limply in their hold, head lolling from side to side.

The clearing was much larger than where they had been captured. Right in the middle, sticking out of the elephant grass, was a tall rock that had been laboriously shaped to resemble a rhino. A heavily bearded man stood on the rock, dressed in the robe and turban of a rhino rider, but with a golden curved rhino horn on a chain around his neck.

Abeke looked at him and then glanced around. There were ranks and ranks of rhino riders behind her. Hundreds of them lined up, riders and rhinos watching the man on the rock, and the prisoners being herded over to him.

"I am Jodoboda!" said the man as Abeke and the others stood before the rock. "Leader of the Tergesh, who you call rhino riders. Speak your names, and hear your doom!"

"I am Lishay, a Greencloak," said Lishay. "We come to—"

"Speak only your names!" roared Jodoboda.

"I am Abeke," said Abeke proudly. "Of Okaihee."

"I am Conor," said Conor. "Of nowhere in particular."

"And your companion?"

"He is Rollan," said Lishay. "He is sick, he needs—"

"Quiet!" roared Jodoboda. "From now on only one of you may speak. I choose . . . you!"

He pointed at Conor. The boy gulped and looked at Lishay, who nodded her head slightly in encouragement.

"Um, we are Greencloaks," said Conor in a hesitant voice. "We don't mean you . . . the rhino riders any harm. We just need to find Dinesh the Elephant."

"We are the Tergesh. Did you know these lands were our lands?"

"Uh, yes, but we hoped we might . . . er . . . sneak across," said Conor.

Abeke tightly clenched her bound fists, but kept her face carefully impassive. She didn't want Jodoboda to see anything other than strength in her. Perhaps that would make up for the mess Conor was making.

"We're in a hurry, you see," Conor went on. "Because the Conquerors, the servants of the Devourer . . . They also want to find Dinesh. They're invading Kho Kensit, and they've already taken over Xin Kao Dai."

"We know this," said Jodoboda. "It is a small point in your favor that you are *not* Conquerors."

"So if it's all right with you," Conor continued, "we'd like permission to keep going, to find Dinesh. And we need help for Rollan. He's obviously sick. . . ."

"The Tergesh do not allow trespassers to travel in our lands unchecked," said Jodoboda. "We cannot allow you to wander aimlessly in your quest for Dinesh."

"Do you know where he is?" blurted out Conor.

"We know," said Jodoboda. "But why should I tell you? Why should I help you in any way?"

"You will help us because a child is dying and the Tergesh are honorable people, not monsters!"

The crowd of rhino riders stirred. The voice had come from among their ranks.

Jodoboda blinked. His thick whiskers bristled.

"Who said that?" he bellowed. "Come forward at once!"

One turbaned figure stepped through the crowd to face the man on the rhino-shaped rock. He was robed from head to foot, and as he stepped free of the riders and joined the prisoners, he tossed his turban aside.

Lishay's face lit up.

"Tarik!" Conor cried. "How did you find us?"

The fierce shriek of a falcon came from above as Essix

plummeted down and swooped over his head, circling once around the clearing. With claws extended, she landed in the grass next to Rollan and stalked over to perch on the unconscious boy's chest.

"What is this?" spluttered Jodoboda. He gestured with both hands, and the circle of riders closed in.

Abeke's relief on seeing Tarik was tempered by the fact that now all of them were surrounded by rhino riders.

"We mean no disrespect," Tarik said with a low bow. "Neither do we wish you any harm. Let us pass and we guarantee no harm will come to you."

"No *harm*? To *me*?" Jodoboda tipped back his head and laughed uproariously as though that was the funniest thing he had ever heard.

His laughter choked into silence as a slight figure rose up behind him, and pressed a knife against his throat.

"As my friend says," Meilin told him, "we offer our guarantee."

Abeke felt her eyes bulge in surprise.

"Meilin!" cried Conor. "What−? How−?"

"You mean no disrespect, you say?" asked Jodoboda in a quiet voice. He seemed surprisingly calm with Meilin's knife at his throat. "But you are standing on the Rock of the People, which is the opposite of respectful. Climb down, and we will talk."

Meilin hesitated, and for the first time caught sight of Rollan on the ground. Her eyes narrowed and her knife moved close enough to Jodoboda's neck to give him a shave.

"What have you done to Rollan?" she cried.

"Nothing!" called out Abeke, her voice calm. "He's sick.

The rhino riders didn't hurt him. Let's all talk peacefully."

Meilin looked at Tarik, who nodded. She hesitated, then slowly put away her knife.

"You see we mean no harm," said Tarik as Meilin climbed down and quickly knelt by Rollan's side, gingerly feeling his forehead with the back of her hand. She looked up at Conor and Abeke. Conor gave her a small wave and Abeke nodded, but that was the extent of their reunion. Proper welcomes and explanations would have to wait until later.

"I do see that now," said Jodoboda, lightly rubbing his throat. "For this, and other reasons, I have decided that we will help you."

"You'll take us to Dinesh and make Rollan well again?" asked Conor.

"No. By ancient custom, we cannot do either of these things, not yet. First, you must complete a task of my choosing. By completing it you will earn the things you ask for."

"This is your way of helping?" asked Meilin, her hand going back to the hilt of her knife.

"What task?" asked Conor with an audible swallow.

Jodoboda fingered his beard, deep-set eyes lingering on Rollan. The boy was very pale, and there were mottled patches of red on his face.

"You must bring me four banana gourds from the deep swamp," he said. "One for each of the Fallen."

"Banana gourds?" asked Conor. "Uh, is that all?"

"'All'? Do you think this task unworthy?"

"You're mocking us!" said Meilin.

"I assure you that I am deadly serious," said Jodoboda sternly. "Your friend has the Sunset Death. The cure is made from the seeds of the banana gourd. If he does not have it before nightfall tomorrow, he will die."

Everyone looked at Rollan. The red blotches on his face were the color of sunset. There were small beads of sweat all over his skin as well, and his breathing was very shallow.

"He's dying?" asked Meilin anxiously. "We must go to the deep swamp at once!"

"Not all of us, I think," said Tarik. "Can Jhi help him? Her healing . . ."

"Oh, of course," said Meilin. There was a bright flash and the panda appeared. Jhi looked down at Rollan, gave a sigh, and began to lick his head. The boy groaned and moved, the first time he had done so since they'd been watching.

"How could you let him get so sick?" asked Meilin, looking up at the others.

"We . . . I . . . didn't notice," said Abeke quietly, feeling shame in the face of Meilin's accusation. "He didn't say anything."

"I should have noticed," said Lishay and Tarik at the same time.

"Jhi is helping him," said Abeke. "Look, the red, it's fading."

Although the bright red rash was retreating a little, it didn't entirely go away.

"Your spirit animal has eased his suffering, but there is only one cure," said Jodoboda. "We are leaving to attend to other matters and will return before sunset tomorrow. Bring the banana gourds here. If you succeed, we will allow you passage to the Lake of the Elephant. Fail, and your friend will die. We will take you to our borders . . . and whatever fate awaits you beyond our lands."

"Where is the deep swamp?" asked Conor.

Jodoboda smiled a grim smile.

"It is *your* task, not mine," he said, and walked away to a waiting rhino. Leaping onto its back, he patted its flank and took hold of a chain that pierced the base of its pointed horn. Jodoboda raised his hand and pointed to the west. A great snorting and bellowing came from the riders, and then they were all in motion at once, leaping onto their leathery steeds and charging out of the clearing, many of them swerving to avoid the small knot of Greencloaks and the great rock.

Tarik freed Abeke and she helped him free the others. Meilin did not move from Rollan's side, her hand on Jhi's neck as the panda continued to slowly lick the boy's head.

"Lishay, do you know where the deep swamp is?" asked Abeke.

"Roughly," answered Lishay. "We'd best get going as soon as we can. Tarik, perhaps you should stay with Rollan and Meilin?"

"I am not sure," said Tarik. "I doubt if the rhino riders have really left this place unguarded. Rollan should be safe enough here with Meilin."

The falcon lifted her head and gave a piercing whistle.

"And with Essix and Jhi, of course," added Tarik. "You may need me – and Lumeo – in the swamp."

"We're only going to get some banana gourds," said Abeke. "How hard can that be?"

No one answered.

"We can't leave yet," said Conor. He was staring at Meilin with pinched intensity. "I have to say . . . I have to know. Meilin . . . why did you come back?"

She stood up and faced him. The air between them crackled with tension, and Abeke instinctively went to intervene. They couldn't fight about *that* again now.

But they didn't fight.

"I . . . I made a mistake," said Meilin. "I shouldn't have left, Conor.

"Oh," said Conor. His ears turned bright red, but he didn't drop his eyes, and for the first time in days he didn't apologize. "I'm glad," he said. "Did you find your father?"

Meilin nodded, then shook her head sharply once. Clearly she didn't want to talk about that.

"I got lost on the way into Zhong. A Marked woman rescued me in the Great Bamboo Maze. I think she used to be a Greencloak. Her name was Xue."

"Xue!" Tarik exclaimed.

"You know her?" asked Meilin.

"I thought she was dead," said Tarik. "Xue left the Greencloaks when I was young. She said there was too much talking and not enough doing."

"And she's right," said Meilin, looking down at Rollan. "Even now, we're too much talking and not enough doing."

"Yes," said Lishay, nodding. "We must go."

Abeke and Conor looked at each other, then back at Meilin. They had only just been reunited, and now they were parting again. It felt . . . not wrong exactly, but dangerous. Tempting fate.

"Good luck," said Meilin, turning back to Rollan and Jhi.

"You too," said Conor. "Look after him."

"We'll be back soon," Abeke promised them all.

11

DANGEROUS WATERS

W E'LL NEED OUR SPIRIT ANIMALS TO GUIDE US FROM here onward," said Tarik, surveying the swamp ahead. For the last hour the ground had been gradually sloping down, and the jungle floor had become wetter and wetter as the trees began to thin. Now they faced open ground with pools of stagnant water lined at the edges with tufts of reeds. Small islands of mud were dotted everywhere, surrounded by thick rafts of clotted weeds. Brightly colored fungus peeked at them from every nook and grotto. Conor didn't recognize any of the species but felt safe assuming they were all deadly.

"Uraza won't like this," said Abeke, calling her spirit animal forth.

"Neither will Briggan," said Conor, doing the same.

"Best to have them ready to help, though," said Lishay. She scratched Zhosur behind the ears and the tiger purred, almost like a house cat, though it was much deeper and three times as loud.

"What do banana gourds grow on?" asked Conor.

"Palmlike trees," said Lishay. "There must be a bigger island somewhere. They wouldn't grow in this part of the swamp."

"I wonder if Briggan could smell a banana gourd tree," said Conor. He bent down by the wolf and looked into his eyes. "Do you know banana gourd trees?"

Briggan licked his face. Conor leaned back, laughing. It was the first time he had laughed for a long time. Meilin's return had released something that had been tied up very tightly inside him.

"I'm not sure if that's a yes. Will you lead the way, Briggan?"

The wolf turned on his tail and set out into the swamp, sniffing the ground and taking a meandering path to the nearest small island.

"I think we should follow him exactly," said Conor. "Unless you want to fall in."

They all waded carefully after Briggan. Zhosur didn't seem to mind the water too much, but Uraza yowled with her first steps, and tried to lift her paws high out of the water.

"It's not that bad," said Abeke. "There's solid ground up ahead. Somewhere."

"And Briggan's doing a great job of finding the way through," said Conor. A moment later the wolf disappeared with a loud splash, reappearing a few seconds later, violently dog-paddling in a circle back to where he'd stepped off.

"I shouldn't have distracted him," said Conor loyally, quickly brushing the mud and slime off the wolf.

"Too much water," said Tarik. "He can't smell the path. This is a job for Lumeo, I think."

Lumeo made a chuckling noise and launched off Tarik's shoulder into the water, flowing into it as if he were liquid himself. He duck-dove several times, sped up and down the line of Greencloaks, and then went ahead, sometimes swimming, sometimes leaping around on the muddy parts.

"Give him a few minutes, and he'll find us a good path ahead," said Tarik.

Lumeo returned and led them on into the swamp. A few miles in they found several larger islands that were higher and drier than the previous mounds of mud. But even when they had trees, none of them turned out to be banana gourd trees.

"It's getting dark," said Conor, looking up at the sky. "We'd better choose an island to camp on."

"I don't think that's a good idea," said Lishay.

"We're not seriously going to walk through this at night, are we?"

"Look," said Tarik, pointing at his spirit animal.

Lumeo was standing up on his hind feet, his head cocked to one side. A moment later, Briggan whined and started to circle around Conor. The two big cats pricked up their ears and both growled simultaneously.

Far off in the distance, they saw the flare of torches, dipping up and down. There was a long line of them, but it was too dark already to see anything but vague shapes behind the flames.

"People with torches, wading," said Tarik. "Strange . . ."

"They're not the rhino riders," said Conor, certain that

Briggan would have recognized their scent.

"I can see something in the water," said Tarik.

Lumeo jumped wetly to Tarik's shoulder. Man and otter peered into the darkness, toward the flickering lights.

"Some things . . . moving fast."

"Could be crocodiles," said Lishay. "But the crocs here are freshwater ones, they aren't very big, and they don't attack humans—"

"Unless they are affected by the Bile," said Tarik bleakly. "They're moving fast, being driven by that line of torchbearers."

"Toward us," said Abeke. "That can be no accident."

"Hadn't we better get on one of these islands, then?" asked Conor nervously. He wouldn't be happy until he was up on dry land.

"Yes, that's our best option," said Tarik. The few bigger islands were already turning into dim silhouettes in the twilight. He pointed to the closest. "Lumeo, find us a way to that one."

Lumeo wasted no time playing around now. The others followed him quickly, relieved to get out of the water and up onto the island. But it was only a few feet above the water, with some sickly palms at the center. There was no real cover, and no defense against crocodiles or the people who were herding them.

"It's very dark," said Conor.

"Try tapping into Briggan's senses," said Tarik. "You too, Abeke. Ask for your spirit animal's help. That's what I do with Lumeo."

"And I with Zhosur," said Lishay. "Not all bonds are the same, but—"

Lishay never finished her sentence, her hand flashing to her sword hilt. There was an abrupt thrashing in the water nearby, and suddenly two huge crocodiles swarmed up the muddy slope of the island. Each was over twelve feet long and swollen with hideous muscle. Their deep-set eyes were red with more than just anger.

These are no spirit animals! thought Conor as the crocodiles charged straight at the Greencloaks.

The two big cats leaped at the closest crocodile. Zhosur jumped over its head with a snarl and fastened his huge jaws on the reptile's left rear leg. Uraza followed a moment later to fasten on to the croc's right. Both hung on, digging their paws into the mud as the croc whipped its tail and writhed backward, trying to snap at them with its three-foot-long, toothy jaw. As it strained to bite them, Tarik sprang forward and thrust his sword two-handed up into the soft parts of its throat.

Briggan confronted the second croc, jumping aside at the last instant as it snapped at him, then jumping again to lead it farther inland, allowing Conor to chop at the croc's hindquarters with his ax.

Abeke, standing calmly where she was, nocked an arrow and sent it at the croc's head. She aimed for the eye, but missed it by a fraction of an inch, the arrow ricocheting off the reptile's thick hide. The croc snapped again at Briggan, ramming into a tree as the wolf ducked aside, only narrowly avoiding losing his tail to the wickedly pointed teeth.

Without even thinking about what he was doing, Conor ran up the crocodile's broad back, balancing precariously on the spiny ridges. The crocodile backed away. Conor almost fell off, but managed to raise his ax over his head and bury it deep into the crocodile's head, just behind its eyes.

To his amazement and horror, that didn't kill it. If anything, it only made it more enraged. The ax remained embedded as it flung its head from side to side, roaring, then rolled completely over. Conor only just jumped aside before it crushed him beneath its bulk.

His ax lost, he drew his knife, though that would be of little use.

The crocodile turned, impossibly tight, and advanced, the ax like some strange crest sticking out of its head. Conor kept his eyes fixed on its furious red glare, ready to dodge aside as it snapped at him.

Then Abeke appeared at his side and sent an arrow at point-blank range into one eye socket and then the next, both of them driven home with such power that they disappeared up to their fletches. The crocodile lurched forward several paces, claws clutching at the mud, then collapsed at their feet.

Tarik came over and helped Conor pull his ax out of the dead croc. Its twisted muscles were still as hard as rock.

"Quickly!" called Lishay, standing on the back of the second croc and surveying the swamp around them. "Cut some staves from the tree and get going. There are more of these vile creatures coming."

Conor's ax came free with a hideous sucking sound. Tarik clapped his hand on Conor's shoulder and went to join Lishay.

"Keep moving along our present course," he said to Conor and Abeke. "We'll lead the other crocodiles away and catch up when we can."

"Is that safe?" Abeke asked.

"Don't worry," said Lishay. "You'll be fine if you stay under cover."

The girl's teeth flashed in the dark. "I meant safe for you."

Tarik grinned in return. He exchanged a look with Lishay, who nodded, then the two of them and their spirit animals raced off to the other side of the island, shouting and splashing as they entered the water. There were answering roars and shouts off in the distance, and Conor and Abeke saw the line of lights from the torchbearers began to move after the older Greencloaks.

"Is it just me, or are they having too much fun?" asked Conor.

"The trust of a good friend is precious," Abeke said. "It makes bearable even the darkest of nights."

Conor shifted awkwardly on his feet. He wasn't sure if she was talking about Tarik and Lishay, or about how he had betrayed Rollan's trust. What if Meilin's return wasn't enough to heal the breach between them? If Rollan died, they might never get the chance to make up. . . .

"Cut some staves for us, as quietly as you can," said Abeke. "Uraza and I will keep watch."

Conor went to the nearest tree and began to cut off some branches, holding the ax close to the head, so he could chip away very quietly. Even though he knew Abeke and Uraza were watching his back, he couldn't help but feel shivers along his spine. Every slight sound made him think a crocodile was about to leap upon him.

He had never cut a pair of staves so quickly. Handing

one to Abeke, they crossed to the far side of the island and began to feel for a path.

"Which way do we go?" asked Conor. He had lost track of the landmarks during the fight.

"That way," said Abeke, pointing. "According to the stars, that is the way we were going. Toward the sign of the Elephant's Trunk, see?"

Conor looked up where she was indicating. A row of stars did suggest the outline of an elephant's trunk, though it was not a constellation he knew.

"Perhaps that's good luck," he whispered, glad that there at least were stars to look at. There were clouds over the swamp, but not so many as in the jungle. He wished the stars provided a little more light, though, so he could see anything creeping up on him.

Briggan nudged his hip to get Conor's attention. He looked down into the wolf's black eyes, wondering what they had picked out of the darkness.

"Wait a moment," he said to Abeke. "Remember what Tarik said about using our animals' senses?"

"Of course!"

She bent down and hugged Uraza. Conor knelt by Briggan's side and did the same.

"Shut your eyes," he said, "and ask."

They shut their eyes, and both mumbled a request to their spirit animals to help them see.

When they opened them again, Conor gasped. He *could* see much more, but it was like the world was lit by a curious bluish light. It wasn't bright enough to cast shadows, but he could see farther across the water.

He also could smell much more, particularly Briggan,

but he could now identify the different smells of the plants nearby, and Uraza, and Abeke, and himself. Conor wrinkled his nose and sneezed, muffling it at the last minute with his hand.

Briggan looked up at him with a tongue-lolling grin, and whuffed as though amused by his reaction.

"Did it work?" asked Abeke.

"Yes," said Conor. "I can smell better too! What about you?"

"I'm not sure," said Abeke slowly. Uraza's head butted hard against hers, rubbing from side to side. "It is lighter, but my eyes feel strange. . . . It will take a bit of getting used to, this ability. I think you should lead, for now."

They waded out, Conor prodding the ground in front and close to either side as he went, with Abeke and the spirit animals reluctantly following. Uraza actually hissed with almost every step, and Briggan growled several times when the water became deeper, or there were reeds and water-weeds to wade through. Conor used his enhanced senses to study the water around him as closely as he followed the stars ahead, but either there was nothing in there or he still couldn't see it.

They walked and waded in this way for several hours, until Conor found himself stepping through shallower water, and slowly they climbed out onto the shores of a much larger island. With his new night sight he could see the dim silhouettes of large trees farther up, but he wasn't sure how far away they were. However, they did offer the hope of finding banana gourds, the first suggestion they had yet had that they were going in the right direction.

"I think we should rest here," he said quietly. As they

moved, the ground beneath them had turned from mud to something like damp earth, the reeds giving way to a softer grass. "We can look for the banana gourds at dawn."

"Yes," said Abeke. "I'll take the first watch."

"Are you sure? Briggan and Uraza can watch for us. You must be as tired as I am, and I can barely stay awake."

"I'm not so tired," said Abeke stiffly, although Conor was sure she really was.

"All right, you take the first watch," he said. There was no shame in admitting to exhaustion. Besides, they would be no help to Rollan or anyone else if they were both so worn out they made mistakes.

Sighing, he lay down in the grass, setting his ax close by his hand. A couple of leeches he hadn't noticed fell off his wrist, bloated with blood. "Uh, can you tell when an hour's up?"

"The stars will tell me," said Abeke.

"Wake me in an hour, then," said Conor. He scratched Briggan's head. The wolf gave a throaty rumble and lay down next to him, a warm and comforting body. A moment later, Conor was fast asleep.

12

ALONE

IT WAS VERY QUIET AFTER EVERYONE LEFT THE CLEARING. Jhi stopped licking Rollan's head, but she lay down next to him and put a paw on his chest, where Essix had been sitting. Essix hopped onto the panda's shoulder, wanting to be higher but not willing to be separated from Rollan.

Meilin's options now were limited. Since the others had left, she'd done little more than pace restlessly around the rhino-shaped rock to make sure there weren't any enemies hiding nearby. Or rhino riders. She wasn't sure if they could be called enemies or not. They certainly weren't allies. She had a suspicion that Jodoboda had been playing a trick on the others, sending them off in search of something that would ultimately prove to be useless. While she stayed behind, feeling useless herself.

My hope lies with you, her father had said. How was she helping him now, sitting here doing nothing? Sometimes she wished someone *would* attack, just so she would have something to do.

She came back to Rollan and looked down at him. Jhi's healing powers had lessened the red rash on his face, but he still looked very sick. She didn't want to imagine what would happen if Jodoboda's so-called cure didn't work.

"I hope those banana gourd seeds help you, Rollan," she said, unable to keep the tension from her voice, then jumped as the boy suddenly opened one eye, just a crack.

"Blo doo hi," he whispered. It took her a moment to work out he'd said, *"So do I."*

Meilin knelt by his side.

"Do you need some water?"

Rollan shook his head slightly. He still only had one eye half open.

"Oog aim vack," he said, which she correctly interpreted as *"You came back."*

"Don't talk," she said. "Save your strength."

"Cold," said Rollan. The word was quite clear. Meilin frowned. It was as hot as ever in the jungle clearing. But she saw Rollan's pack nearby, so she got a blanket from it and wrapped him up in it.

"Is that better?" she asked anxiously, but Rollan did not reply. Jhi stirred and leaned across, then started to lick the boy's head again.

Essix looked at her, and Meilin wondered what else she could or should do to help him. Rollan's life had been entrusted to her, but something more than pride drove her to want to help him. He was unruly and impulsive, and his sense of duty was very different from hers. He still hadn't agreed to become a Greencloak! But she had no doubt that in her shoes he would think of something to make her feel better, even if it was just to make her laugh. Or try to.

Sometimes he could be so annoying. . . .

A faint noise came from one of the nearby clumps of elephant grass. Immediately she stood up, her staff ready. The tops of the grass were waving – perhaps caused by something as innocent as a breath of wind, or by stealthy movement of something coming toward them.

Essix launched from Jhi's shoulder with a screech, shot up to a height of about a hundred feet, and hovered there, watching whoever or whatever it was that was approaching.

Essix didn't screech a warning or dive to attack, but even so, Meilin's grip on her staff tightened and she adopted a defensive stance, ready for whatever might spring out of the elephant grass.

It wasn't a tiger and it didn't leap.

It was Xue, with her towering pack, the old woman hunched over beneath it. She emerged from the taller grass and walked toward Meilin.

"Xue! I didn't expect to see you again!"

"Why not?" asked Xue.

"Um, I . . . I just didn't," said Meilin. "What are you doing here?"

"Selling pots to the Tergesh," said Xue. She set her pack down and slowly straightened out, her hands on her hips. "They gather here, this time of year. Or they usually do," she added, looking around at the empty grass.

"They're coming back," said Meilin. "Tomorrow. My friends have gone to complete a task set by their leader, Jodoboda."

"The Tergesh and their tasks!" said Xue. She bent down and looked at Rollan. A second later, Essix landed near her and hopped onto Rollan's chest.

"Oh, this one's yours, is he, Essix?" asked Xue. "Sunset Death. Not good. You have any banana gourd seeds?"

"No," said Meilin. "Are they really a cure? The others have gone to get some. . . ."

"Part of the cure," said Xue. "He is unlucky to have caught it. Insect bite gone wrong. We need to move him near the rock."

"Why?" asked Meilin.

"Rain," said Xue, pointing at the sky. She pointed at the rock. "We'll take shelter there."

"The rain's warm," said Meilin doubtfully. "Should he be moved?"

"Won't feel warm to him," said Xue. She opened the top of her pack and rummaged around inside, pulling out a tightly folded square of oiled silk, some light cord, and several tent pegs. Going over to the rock, she quickly erected a shelter, tying the waterproof fabric off to the horn and pegging the other end down.

"You take his legs," she said to Meilin, going to Rollan's head and lifting him under the shoulders. "Essix, you fly. Too heavy."

Surprisingly, Essix did exactly as Xue said, flying off to perch on the rhino horn on the rock, while Meilin and Xue carried Rollan to the shelter. Jhi ambled after them and pushed her way under the makeshift tent next to Rollan, leaving no room for anyone else.

"Ha!" cackled Xue. "The panda is lazy . . . and a water-shirker."

They had barely gotten Rollan settled when the shower suddenly began, not with any preliminary drops, but a full-on deluge, as if high above someone had just over-turned a giant bucket. Meilin crouched with her back against the rock, which didn't really do anything to stop the rain but felt like it might help somehow. Xue dragged her pack over, rummaged in it again, and produced a beautiful waxed-paper umbrella, illustrated with pictures of a dancing mouse. It was evidently modeled on her spirit animal, who was either in the dormant state or lurking in his special pocket.

"Tarik . . . the senior Greencloak with us," said Meilin hesitantly. "He said that he'd heard of you. You retired from the Greencloaks years and years ago. . . . Is that true?"

"Greencloaks rarely retire," said Xue. "I took a long leave of absence. Probably time to come back. The younger ones are not so well-trained."

"Well, we've only just started," protested Meilin. "And we haven't done too badly. We've gotten the Granite Ram, and even though we lost the Iron Boar, there was . . . an understandable reason for that—"

Xue laughed a short, high-pitched laugh.

"Not you! Olvan, Lenori. Always forgetting my lessons."

"Oh?" said Meilin, wondering at the thought that Olvan and Lenori were once students like her. And bad students at that. It was impossible to imagine!

"We should make fire for tea," said Xue, not letting herself be drawn on the subject. "Collect dry rhino dung before it gets too wet. There are piles of it near the jungle edge, under trees."

"I'll go," said Meilin, jumping to her feet, water cascading off her shoulders where it had gathered.

"Yes," said Xue.

Five minutes later, as she gathered the driest rhino dung she could find, Meilin wondered why she had volunteered so readily. She would never have dreamed back home that she would ever do something like collect dung, even if the dry pieces really just felt like pieces of light wood.

But she wanted Xue to respect her, and the only way to do that was to do what needed to be done.

Even if it was something like collecting dung for a fire.

At least she didn't feel quite so trapped now. She had someone to talk to whose words she didn't have to think twice about before understanding them.

She smiled. That was the kind of thing Rollan might have said.

The rain eased off as she walked back, and then it stopped abruptly. The clouds edged apart, and Meilin caught a glimpse of the setting sun through the western tree line. Under Xue's direction, she stacked the dry dung in a pyramid in the lee of the rock, some distance from the shelter. Xue lit it with a twisted piece of oily paper and a clockwork fire starter, a beautifully enameled egg in two halves that had to be turned fifteen times. It would not have been out of place in her father's treasure cabinet, Meilin thought.

Xue rigged up her tripod and cooking pot, and made tea. After they drank their own, Meilin took some of the cooled tea and spooned it into Rollan's mouth. After several tries she got him to swallow some, but he wasn't really conscious, and he did not speak again.

"You're good to care for him," the old woman said with an approving nod.

"Who else is going to do it?" Meilin said with a frustrated sigh.

"Caring takes many forms."

"You mean there's something else I should be doing?"

"No." Xue squinted with one eye, but the other was wide open. "*You* know. Loneliness is a kind of death too."

Meilin looked away, not really understanding but feeling as though Xue was seeing her with a clarity that made her uncomfortable.

"Jodoboda said he will die by tomorrow's sunset unless he has the cure," Meilin said, to bring the conversation back on track.

"This is true," said Xue. She took a jar of rice out of her pack, some dried meat that was probably rat, and several herb containers, and began to prepare dinner. "But not until then. After dinner, we sleep. The animals will keep watch. Zap too."

She opened the top of her jacket. The jumping mouse lived up to his name by jumping out. He ran over to Meilin, who held out her hand. He climbed into it and she lifted him up near her face to see him better in the twilight. He was entirely white, but did not have an albino's red eyes. His eyes were deep, and very knowing.

"I used to think only the big, fierce spirit animals were any good," Meilin confessed, carefully setting Zap back down. He jumped over to Jhi and sat near her front paw, like some small retainer sitting before the empress.

"Big, small, doesn't matter," said Xue. "It's a spirit animal! Not a simple animal. True strength is unrelated to size or fierceness."

"I guess I'm getting to know that," said Meilin with a glance at Jhi.

"True bonds test us," Xue said with a nod, collecting up their empty bowls. "Sleep now."

Meilin looked at Rollan, thinking of his sharp wit and how, even though he hadn't taken any vows, he had stayed when she had not. She realized for the first time that she thought of him not just as an equal, but as a friend. She hadn't ever really had any friends before. Just servants and the children of officers lower ranking than her father.

"Is there really nothing else I can do?"

Xue shook her head. "Tell me your dreams, later, if you have any strange ones."

"Will they . . . tell the future?"

"No. I like a good story."

Meilin forced herself to lean back against the rock. It was too wet to lie down, but some of the warmth from the fire reached her. She was restless and tired at the same time. She watched Rollan lying with the spirit animals, his breath shallow. It was awful, being so helpless, knowing that unless Abeke and Conor and the others got back in time with the banana gourd seeds, he would die. But he wasn't alone, and neither, now, was she.

"I shouldn't have gone away," she whispered, as much to Rollan as to herself, although she knew he couldn't hear her. "I won't make that mistake again."

13

TALL TREES AND THORNBUSHES

ABEKE WOKE UP WITH A START. THE FIRST FAINT LIGHT OF dawn was falling on their sleeping spot in the grass. Conor was slumped on his side nearby, curled up next to Briggan. The wolf looked at her with ears standing straight upright. Uraza was sitting on her haunches next to him, licking mud from her fur.

Abeke's breath caught in her throat. She hadn't woken Conor to take his watch. In fact, she had nodded off and fallen asleep through her watch as well. They had been completely exposed, and it was her fault!

She staggered up and looked around. They were on a large island, all right, and the big trees were *really* tall palm trees, the smallest easily a hundred feet high. They were all lined up along a central ridge several hundred yards away, and perhaps a hundred feet higher, well out of the swampy ground.

Best of all, she could see they had bunches of some kind of curvy fruit hanging from the upper branches. They had to be banana gourds!

She went off a little way to think very hard about what to do. She could lie and tell Conor that she had let him sleep, or she could confess and tell him the truth about what had happened. She called herself a hunter of the Niloan savannah, yet she had fallen asleep on her watch!

When she returned, Conor was muttering in his sleep, as if he was having a nightmare.

"The sheep! We'll never get them all in! What are you doing? No, not that way! No, not that way!"

She crouched down next to him and touched his shoulder. He sat bolt upright with eyes wide open, panting.

"You were having a bad dream," she said.

"I was," he said, looking around him. "The flock . . . there was a . . ." His eyes fell on Briggan, and he reached out to hug the wolf. "Wait, the sun's up. What happened to our agreement? Why did you let me sleep?"

How easy it would be to lie, she thought. *He* trusts *me*.

"I dropped off without realizing," she said, prepared for his anger. "That was why I didn't wake you up. I was asleep too. I'm sorry."

He nodded gravely. "So Uraza kept watch, with Briggan?"

"Yes."

"I don't see the problem." He smiled at her. "They would have woken us if anything had come near. Don't worry. I won't tell anyone. Okay?"

She hesitated, and then said, "Okay."

He stood up and looked at the sun, the swamp, and the trees, in that order.

"I don't suppose there's time for breakfast," he said, not sounding terribly hopeful.

"We've only got till nightfall to find the banana gourds and get them back to Jodoboda," Abeke said, standing up and stowing her bow and arrows. "We can eat while we walk."

"I guess so." He rubbed at the sleep still crusting his eyes, and Briggan yawned in sympathy, white teeth and red gums gleaming in the morning light. "These banana gourds had better work."

Abeke didn't speak. She hoped Jodoboda was telling the truth about a cure for Rollan. She also hoped that Tarik and Lishay were all right, and that they had managed to lead the crocodiles far away. Because getting the banana gourds was one thing. Returning with them to the rhino riders across the swamp might be another altogether.

The ridge was higher than it looked, and it was more difficult to get to the palm trees than the two Greencloaks had anticipated. Halfway up the slope there were thorn-bushes blocking their way, and even Briggan and Uraza could not find a way through them, so they had to walk along and look for a gap. When they eventually did find one, it led into another wall of thorny hedges.

"This is a maze," said Conor. "Like that bamboo one Meilin said she went through."

"That's much bigger," replied Abeke. "Huge. This is small. I believe these are called snarevines."

"It's going to slow us down for sure," said Conor gloom-ily. "And we can't waste any time."

"There might be a way," Abeke said. She pointed to the nearest tree. It was about twenty yards away, across the tangle of thornbushes, and perhaps twenty feet up the slope. "What if one of us used the Granite Ram to jump to the lowest branch on that tree?"

Conor looked up and frowned.

"Across thorns? If it didn't work . . . and even if it did, those branches don't look strong."

"We have to try," said Abeke. "There isn't time to walk along the snarevine bushes, hoping to find a way in."

"You're right," he said slowly. "Let me do it."

Abeke shook her head. She took off her pack and laid her bow on top of it.

"I'm the best jumper, and I was the last one to practice with the Granite Ram," she said. "Uraza will help me too."

"I can do it," Conor insisted. "I won't let you down."

Abeke shook her head again.

"It's not that. Yes, I was angry with you, over the Iron Boar . . . but we've all made mistakes. I made one last night."

"Mine was a particularly big one," he started to say.

"If a crocodile had crept up on us last night, mine would have been pretty big too. We could be dead now, not arguing about who's most at fault."

He looked down at his feet, then back up at her.

"All right, then," he said. "You are the best jumper . . . and we have no time for second chances."

Abeke looked up at the tree and the thornbushes in between. She would have to do a standing jump, over the high thorns, up twenty feet and across about sixty, grab that branch there . . . which would probably break, but it would slow her down and she could drop from there to the ground. But she couldn't see the ground. There could be anything there. More thorns, sharp stones, anything . . .

Uraza grumbled at her side. Abeke rested her hand on the leopard's head.

"I'll need your help," she said. "You and the Ram."

Uraza's tail twitched, but the grumbling stopped. Abeke felt strength flow into her, strength and the feline grace of the big cat, energizing her muscles. She touched the Granite Ram that hung on its chain around her neck, and drew on its power too.

Then she jumped, and the earth seemed to fall away beneath her.

Conor's whistle followed her as she flew through the air, high over the thorns. The whistle faltered when she reached the highest point of her incredible leap and it looked like she was going to miss the tree. Conor was forgotten as she flailed wildly for a branch on the way down, missed grabbing it properly, but slowed herself enough to spin end over end and land belly-first on the next branch down.

Winded, it was all she good do to hang on, relieved that she had at least come to a halt. She rocked backward and forward for a few seconds, raising one hand to wave at Conor to let him know that she was okay. Then, with a horrible tearing noise, the branch came away from the tree.

For the briefest moment Abeke was suspended. Then she fell, hands desperately clawing the air for a hold that was no longer there.

"Abeke!" shouted Conor. Uraza yowled.

Fortunately the base of the tree was home to only

young vines, so the thorns she landed on merely pricked her, rather than causing her serious harm. She lay among them, catching her breath, then called out to reassure Conor and Uraza so they wouldn't try to follow her.

"I'm all right! I'll go back up in a minute."

The tree looked much taller than it had from down below. It also looked much higher than the mainmast of the *Tellun's Pride*, though at least it wasn't swaying from side to side. The bark of the trunk was rough, with sufficient handholds to get her to the first branch. Once she was breathing properly, she reached up and took a firm grip. Staying close to the trunk, she climbed carefully until the first branch was within reach, then just as carefully tested its weight. It held, so she transferred herself and pulled herself up.

From there she climbed carefully from branch to branch, quickly learning that the branches would come away if she planted her feet wrong and put too much weight on them.

"I see you!" called Conor when she ascended into view. "You're doing great!"

Abeke didn't turn to look. Just thinking of him so far below her made her falter.

She touched the Granite Ram again.

"Save me if I fall," she whispered, and then felt a little ashamed to be so fearful. If she didn't think about the thorns below or her steadily increasing altitude, and if she concentrated hard on where she put her hands and feet, she would be fine.

So she told herself, and so it was. After an ascent that seemed to last hours, she looked up and she saw a cluster of the banana-shaped gourds hanging halfway along a branch, slightly farther around the tree. There were six of the gourds there, two more than she needed. But she couldn't reach them yet.

Abeke started to edge around as she climbed, going faster with the gourds now in sight. They were too far along the branch to reach, but she thought if she could break the branch off, they would fall to the ground. As she knew from her own fall, the vines were thick down there; the gourds should survive the descent.

But the branch wouldn't break off. Abeke tugged at it and twisted it, but it simply wouldn't come away from the trunk. The gourds didn't fall off either, as she had hoped they might.

Abeke stopped working on the branch. There was another bunch of gourds higher up, and a little closer to the trunk. Maybe she could reach out and pull them off, one by one. She gave the branch another resentful tug, but when that didn't work, started to climb again.

She was now at least fifty feet above the ground, and the higher branches were crackling under her feet, as if they were even more precarious than the ones lower down. Abeke started to climb faster, a little less carefully. She wanted to spend less time on each branch, giving it fewer chances to fail.

One cracked completely as she climbed, and she would have fallen if she had not leaped for the next. Shocked by the sudden noise and the lurch underneath her, Abeke accelerated again. Reaching the branch with the gourds, she leaned out and plucked them off incredibly quickly, letting them fall to the ground. One, two, three, four, and then another one for luck, and she was on her way, climbing back down, trying to keep hold with at least one hand every time she moved her feet.

She got to within twenty-five feet of the ground and was feeling incredibly relieved when disaster struck. Two branches broke at once, one under her hand and one under her foot. The crack of them breaking mixed with her shout as she fell backward from the tree.

Abeke plummeted. The chain holding the Granite Ram slipped over her head. It caught on her nose and for a frenzied second held there, as she crossed her eyes, staring at it and willing it to stay.

But it didn't, falling away with all the finality of a shooting star that will never be seen again.

Uraza yowled below, and with it Abeke felt a burst of unexpected power. Somehow she pivoted while falling, exactly like a cat, and hooked one leg over a lower branch. So gracefully she surprised even herself, she swung around the branch, grabbed another, and then swung to a third, making an astonishingly swift and acrobatic descent to the ground.

There, she searched anxiously among the vines for the Granite Ram, her heart pounding. If she'd lost it . . . that would be the second talisman gone. Conor at least had a reason to give away the Iron Boar. Just losing a talisman out of carelessness would be much worse. . . .

Then she saw the glint of the chain, draped across one of the fallen gourds. She put a hand to her throat and breathed again. Gathering up the Granite Ram, she slipped it over her head and knotted the chain to shorten it. There was no way that talisman would come off again!

It took her several minutes longer to find the gourds. In the end, she could only find four of the five. The fifth one must have rolled away, lost in the snarevine thorns.

"I've got four!" she shouted, tying them up in her shirt and buttoning her sailor's jacket over the top. "I'm going to climb up and jump to you."

Conor's anxious shout came back. "Be careful!"

Abeke retraced her slow ascent up the tree, more painfully than the first time, her muscles aching from the previous exertion and with numerous small bruises from her fall. She concentrated on moving very patiently. She would need all her strength, plus the powers of the talisman and her spirit animal, to make the leap back over the thorns safely.

Uraza clearly felt the risk too. When Abeke rose up above the vines and could see her again, the leopard was pacing backward and forward, continually looking up toward the tree and Abeke.

"Don't move!" called out Abeke when she was about thirty feet up. "I don't want to land on you!"

Uraza stopped and settled on her haunches. Conor stood perfectly still, Briggan at his side. Abeke looked down at them, held her breath, and jumped.

14

HOPE

MEILIN WATCHED THE SUN, AND THE SHADOW IT CAST from the horn of the rhino rock. Rollan hadn't said anything since complaining about the cold. Occasionally he shivered, as he was shivering now. His teeth chattered.

"It's the second hour of the afternoon," she said. As the day grew old, her patience with waiting grew short. "Maybe I should go and try to find them."

"They will come," said Xue.

Meilin turned to look at the old woman.

"Do you know that for sure?" she asked. "You're certain they'll be back with the banana gourds in time?"

"Yes."

"How? Have you had a vision or something?"

Xue shook her head. "I don't have visions. Just hope."

"Hope!" said Meilin. "Hoping won't do anything."

"So go," said Xue. "I'm not stopping you."

"What?" This Meilin couldn't believe. Xue would let her abandon Rollan and head off into the jungle on what might possibly be a fruitless quest . . . ?

Then she caught herself and realized that even she wasn't convinced that it was the right thing to do.

But what else *could* she do?

Jhi had been watching over Rollan the whole time, alternating between licking his head and placing a paw on his chest. At first, the violently red rash on his face had faded, but now it was even brighter and had spread down his neck and behind his ears. His breathing was becoming increasingly ragged.

Her heart ached in sympathy, as though she were coming down with something too.

She knew she couldn't stay and watch him die.

"You'll really let me go?" she asked Xue, wondering if this was some kind of trick.

"Of course. Too comfortable to get up."

That had to be a lie. Even with the grass to sit on, the ground was hard.

"Then . . . I *will* go. Will you stay and look after Rollan?"

"Not going anywhere," said Xue. "Got to sell some pots to the Tergesh."

"Jhi, you should stay too," said Meilin.

"The panda is too lazy to leave," laughed Xue. "Except as a tattoo."

Xue's nonchalance made Meilin feel slightly foolish, but she was determined to go now that she had come to a decision. If Xue was trying to talk her out of going by *not* talking her out of going, that simply wouldn't work.

"I'll go as far as the swamp," said Meilin. "I might be able to see them from there."

She picked up her staff and looked down at Rollan. The

shivering had ceased for the moment. It left him looking completely lifeless, or nearly so.

"Are you *sure* there's nothing else we can do for him?" she asked.

Xue shook her head, all levity lost.

"I'll be back before nightfall," said Meilin. "With the others. And the banana gourds."

Xue smiled again.

"See? Hope is good. Powerful."

Meilin didn't feel very powerful, but that was all she had.

At the edge of the clearing she looked back, feeling a mental tug. It was strange going off into the jungle without Jhi. They hadn't been separated since the ceremony that had joined them together. The panda lifted her head to look at her, and their eyes met.

"Look after him," whispered Meilin.

Xue turned her head as if she'd heard the whisper, which was impossible. Meilin blushed and looked away, the sensation uncomfortable. She never blushed, and there was no reason to blush now. Was there?

Jhi bent down to Rollan again, and Meilin strode off into the jungle.

15

SUNSET

ABEKE *ALMOST* MADE IT. SHE FELL SLIGHTLY SHORT AND landed on the very edge of the thorn trees, crashing through them to tumble onto the path near Conor, one sleeve already bloody from where the thorns had ripped through her coat and shirt, and the skin beneath.

Conor rushed to her side, but Uraza was even faster. The leopard whined and nosed Abeke, who slowly sat up and looked at her arm.

"Is it bad?" asked Conor. He was already tearing off his shirttail to use as a bandage, but he stopped as Abeke held up her hand.

"Just scratches," said Abeke, pulling the torn cloth apart to investigate. "Nothing very deep. And I got the gourds!"

She undid the knotted ends of her shirt and showed Conor the four banana gourds. They didn't look like much, just curved, dry gourds the length of her index finger. Conor picked one up and shook it, the seeds rattling about inside.

"We'd better clean those scratches," said Conor.

Abeke shook her head.

"Dry, clean thorns are better than swampy water," she said, getting to her feet with a visible wince. "We must head straight back to have any chance of getting there before nightfall."

"True," said Conor. "Um, should I carry your pack too?"

"I can manage it," said Abeke. She walked stiffly over to the pack, put the gourds in one of the pockets, and swung it on her back. Bending again slowly, she picked up her bow and staff, and began to hobble down to the swamp, Uraza following at her heels.

Conor looked at Briggan, who cocked his head sideways and let his tongue loll out.

"I know, I know, she's way tougher than me," said Conor with resignation.

Striking back across the swamp in the daytime rather than at night following the stars, they had to depend on the sun for direction, and on Briggan. But clouds, with occasional downpours of rain, kept obscuring the sun, and the swampy water was too deep for Briggan to easily find a trail. So Conor poked ahead with his staff, checking with Briggan every now and then that they were at least headed in the right general direction.

It was slow going and very tiring, wading through water and reeds, or clomping over muddy banks. Both Conor and Abeke simply couldn't go any faster, no matter how much they urged each other on. Their will was strong, but their bodies were just too tired.

Conor couldn't see the sun, but he knew it was going

down. He tried to increase the pace, lifting his feet higher out of the sucking mud. Rollan didn't have forever: If they took too long or got lost, he would die.

Then they saw the crocodiles. Six of them, huge beasts much larger than any normal freshwater crocodiles that should populate the area. They were lying on the muddy shores of one of the low islands that dotted the swamp.

"Crocs!" warned Conor, hunkering down among the reeds, the water coming up to his armpits. Abeke did the same. Briggan and Uraza tensed beside their companions, quiet so as not to draw attention to them, but ready to spring into action if needed.

"We have to try to sneak around," whispered Abeke.

Conor stood up and swapped his probing staff for the ax on his back. If he had to fight his way past crocs to get the gourds back to Rollan, then so be it. He wished Tarik and Lishay were with them, but there had been no sign of the Greencloaks since they had parted the previous day.

"There are too many to sneak past," he said. "But if I rush them . . . I'll distract them while you run."

Abeke was still staring, her sharp hunter's eyes intent on the crocs.

"I think they're dead," said Abeke. "Look, one is on its back. Crocs never sleep on their backs like that."

"Maybe these monstrous ones do," said Conor. But he felt a momentary hope.

They edged forward, Conor holding his ax ready to strike. As he neared the bodies, he saw that Abeke was correct. The crocs were lying absolutely still, at odd angles, their muscles straining even in death, twisting their legs and tails into tortured shapes.

"Maybe Tarik and Lishay killed them," whispered Conor.

Abeke shook her head.

"No wounds, no blood."

"Oh, right," said Conor.

They drew nearer and nearer. At the waterline, Briggan and Uraza ran ahead, both of them sniffing at the bodies. Briggan recoiled and shook his head.

"Look at their eyes," said Conor.

The crocs were already starting to smell. Their eyes had bulged out of their sockets and there was a black froth coming out of their noses.

"I think they were given Bile," Abeke said. She hesitated, then added, "I saw this being done once. When I was with Shane and Zerif. Men fed what must have been Bile to animals, and squabbled over how much to use. I think it reacts differently when animals drink it. They don't then bond with a human. They become enslaved monsters."

"You saw it!" exclaimed Conor.

"I didn't see what happened when too much was given," said Abeke. "They transformed a dog, a nice dog called Admiral. They made it into a vicious monster, much bigger than it was originally. They must still be experimenting. . . . The Bile is a poison that has to be stopped!"

"It will be," said Conor. "I hope. Come on. Rollan's waiting. We *have* to go faster."

* * *

"Solid ground at last," said Conor wearily, some hours later, as they staggered out of the swampy water and onto the muddy shore of the jungle fringe. "I'm even glad to be heading back into the jungle."

Abeke turned anxious eyes to the sun. "We're too late," she said bitterly. "We'll never make it to the clearing in time."

Conor looked up at the sky. The clouds had come back, but the faint disc of the sun could just be seen, a splash of orange behind the gray. It was already beginning to set.

They had failed. Despite their heroic efforts, they could never get back to the rhino rock in time. The two Greencloaks were exhausted, and even though it was easier than the swamp, the jungle was difficult to make their way through. Walking was hard enough, let alone running. All he could think about was Rollan waiting for them, feverish and ill, perhaps dying at that very moment.

Conor stopped, ankle-deep in the mud.

"Don't just stand there!" croaked Abeke, struggling on. "We can't give up now!"

"I'm not giving up," said Conor angrily. He was very tired and wet and irritable, and he knew everywhere below his thighs was covered in leeches, even though he couldn't feel them. "I'm thinking! We should send the gourds ahead with Briggan and Uraza."

The two spirit animals turned to look at him.

"They can hold two each in their mouths," said Conor. "They can go much faster than us."

Abeke stared at him. She was almost too exhausted to understand what he'd said.

"What if the rhino riders don't consider the task completed unless we do it?" she asked.

"We have to risk it," said Conor. "Surely they'll still make the cure for Rollan?"

"I don't like the idea of Uraza being . . . away from me," said Abeke.

"I don't like Briggan being away either," said Conor. "But it's our only chance of getting the gourds there on time. It's *Rollan's* only chance!"

Uraza put one strong paw on Abeke's knee, as though to support Conor's opinion. Her proud head tilted to one side.

"Yes, of course, you're right," said Abeke. She swung her pack off her back to get the banana gourds out. Uraza and Briggan came up to her. Each took two of the gourds gently in their jaws.

Conor hugged Briggan tightly. "I know you can do it," he said. The wolf's bark was muffled but firm, as though to say, *Of course we can!*

The two spirit animals sprang away, moving far more swiftly than the two children could have managed.

"Come on," said Conor when Briggan and Uraza were out of sight. "We've still got a long way to go."

He pulled his feet out of the mud with a sucking, popping sound.

Another sound came from behind, a chilling slither. For the briefest moment Conor thought it was Abeke moving. Then he knew it was not.

He spun around. Abeke crashed into him, leaping away from a huge, red-eyed crocodile that had slid up the muddy shore like an arrow shot out from under the water. It lunged at Conor, its massive jaws snapping at his leg.

Just before they closed, Conor thrust his staff in the way. The staff snapped in half, but held long enough for him to get his leg clear of the sharp teeth and stagger backward, leaving him holding only a broken tree branch to face an eighteen-foot-long Bile-enraged crocodile.

Abeke didn't have time to get her bow. She snatched an arrow from her quiver and held it like a dagger, stabbing at the crocodile's eyes from the side. Before she could find her mark, it whipped its head across and sent her flying. She landed in the mud ten feet away.

Conor tossed the broken staff into the croc's gaping mouth and reached back for his ax, but he was stuck in the mud and his pack had ridden up. He couldn't quite reach the haft of the ax strapped to the outside, and the croc was advancing once more, its jaws opening again.

"Ha!"

Meilin's shout echoed out across the swamp as she brought her metal-bound staff down on the croc's head. It swung to snap at her, giving Conor a precious few seconds to stagger away and fumble his ax free.

Thwack! Thwack! Thwack! Meilin danced backward across the mud and onto dry land, the crocodile following her, roaring and thrashing its tail. Abeke strung her bow to hasten after the crocodile, followed by the mud-smeared Conor, his ax now held steadily in both hands. Meilin leaped onto the stump of a giant fallen tree, and the crocodile reared against it, gouging at the rotten timber with its claws and snapping at Meilin's feet.

As the crocodile reared at Meilin, Abeke sent an arrow down its gullet. Conor swept the ax fast and low across the beast's throat, silencing it.

The crocodile rolled away and thrashed a trail of bloody destruction halfway across the mudbank toward the open water before it finally died. Blood streamed from its many wounds, dark rivulets spreading across the brown mud.

Abeke sat down where she stood and let out a sigh that was half exhaustion and half relief. Conor stood next to her, leaning on his ax. Meilin jumped down, not looking tired at all.

"Where did you come from?" Conor asked her.

"I came looking for you," she said. "When I saw Briggan and Uraza, I knew you must be close. Then I heard the croc. It was huge! Have you seen many like this?"

Abeke nodded somberly. "You know, General Gar's crocodile, the one I saw . . . It was about twice as long."

Conor shuddered. Even Meilin looked uneasy.

"Thanks, Meilin," he said. "We'd better get moving. Briggan and Uraza have the banana gourds, but they'll be no use to Rollan if he's alone."

"He's not," said Meilin. They exchanged stories as they set off. The sun was no longer visible behind the jungle trees, though the sky was still streaked with sunset colors. All Conor's thoughts were with Briggan and Uraza. He hoped they would make it in time.

16

RETURN OF THE RHINO RIDERS

IT WAS FULLY DARK BY THE TIME MEILIN, ABEKE, AND Conor finally reached the clearing. It was a different place from the one Meilin had left. Bright paper lanterns suspended from long bamboo poles lit up the area. Tents had been pitched in rings around the rhino rock, each with a rhino standing beside it, tethered to a thick iron peg hammered deep into the ground. The riders themselves were gathered around several large fires, eating, drinking, and talking.

Jodoboda was standing on the rhino rock, a golden goblet in his hand. Xue's shelter was gone, and Meilin could not see Rollan. There were too many rhinos and tents in the way. She started to walk faster, though for the last hour she had kept her pace to match the worn-out Conor and Abeke.

He can't be dead, she thought, her heart racing. *Uraza*

and Briggan must have gotten here before sunset. Rollan has to be alive!

She started to run between the tents and rhinos, fearing what she might see, already imagining Rollan's lifeless body on the grass, Essix crazed and hooded, bound with jesses on her feet like any tame falcon gone feral. . . .

Jodoboda raised his goblet and gestured at the ground near the rock. Meilin slowed and schooled her face into its customary calm as she saw Xue sitting on her pack, a porcelain cup in her hand. And there was Jhi next to her, a welcome sight. And next to the panda there was . . .

Rollan, sitting up and grinning like an idiot, his face already a healthier pink. Essix was on his shoulder, preening her feathers. Briggan and Uraza sat next to Rollan, but they both leaped up as their companions came hurrying behind Meilin, and bounded over to greet them.

She walked forward, not saying anything until she could trust her voice not to catch. Her throat felt full and tight with unexpected emotion.

"So they made the cure for you," she said. "I'm glad."

"Not half as much as I am!" Rollan grinned up at her, and Meilin couldn't help but blush. Confused by her emotion, she lowered her chin, watching him from under her eyelashes. She'd thought she'd never see that smile again.

"Xue told me I would be dead if you hadn't gotten the seeds to Jodoboda in time," he said. "Thank you."

"It wasn't me," said Meilin. "It was Conor and Abeke."

Conor and Abeke came up to stand on either side of her.

"We never would have gotten the gourds," said Conor, "if Abeke hadn't done those jumps."

126

Abeke shrugged. "I jumped, but Conor led. It doesn't matter who did what."

"Wise girl," said Xue, introducing herself to the curious Conor and Abeke. Zap poked his head out of her jacket and wiggled his whiskers at them in welcome.

"All I want to do is sit down, eat, and then wash myself off," continued Abeke. "In that order!"

"A full belly makes you strong," said Xue. "We should all eat."

Meilin ignored her. She needed to say something important to the others.

"Jodoboda would never have captured you if I hadn't left," Meilin said. It was the closest thing to an apology anyone had ever heard from her. "Maybe you wouldn't have gotten sick either."

"I would have," said Rollan, his expression pretending seriousness. "Those insects just couldn't resist me!"

"But we would have seen how sick you were if we had been paying attention to each other," said Abeke. "We were so busy being angry at Conor that we weren't noticing the really important stuff."

"We work well together, when we do," said Conor with a bright smile. "Remember the puppet plan? We all came up with that, although we didn't realize at the time. If you had been there, Meilin, it would've been even better."

Meilin nodded. Abeke had told her how the three of them had snuck into Xin Kao Dai. It had been a good plan. Even Rollan seemed to agree.

"I think we've learned our lesson," she said.

"Already better students than Olvan and Lenori," said Xue with a quick wink.

The four children smiled at each other for a moment, then Abeke looked up at the leader of the rhino riders, tall and proud on his rock.

"Thank you for honoring our agreement and making the cure, Jodoboda."

"I would have made it anyway," said Jodoboda, raising his golden mug to her. "We keep many banana gourd seeds. The Sunset Death is not uncommon among my people."

"What!" exclaimed Conor. "We almost got killed getting those gourds!"

"It was your task," said Jodoboda. "I consider it completed, and your true reward will be as you asked. When your other companions return, we will show you how to find the Lake of the Elephant, and Dinesh."

"They're not back yet?" asked Abeke. "Where are they?"

"You do not know?" said Jodoboda.

Rollan looked up in alarm. "Where did they go?"

Abeke quickly told them about the monstrous crocodiles and the line of torchbearers who had driven them toward the Greencloaks. Jodoboda leaned down to listen, a frown on his leathery face.

"This is ill news," he said when Abeke finished. "A force of Conquerors in the swamp, feeding poison to the crocodiles . . . I had not thought they could be here in strength. Pharsit Nang has always been left in peace. *We* have been left in peace. . . ."

"A stone alone is just a stone," said Xue. "Many together can make a wall."

Jodoboda smiled, but it was not a happy smile.

"So you have said before, Old Mother. But the rhino

riders have always stood alone."

"Hidebound," said Xue with a sniff.

"We have to find Tarik and Lishay," said Rollan, struggling to stand.

Xue put a hand on his shoulder and kept him down.

"We'll go," said Conor, though it clearly took all his strength to get the words out.

"*I'll* go," said Meilin, thinking of Tarik and Lishay wounded in the swamp, or besieged by crocodiles. . . .

"No," said Jodoboda. "You have all done enough for now, even for Greencloaks. I will send riders to search for them . . . and to gauge the true extent of the Conquerors in our territory."

He jumped off the stone and stalked out, calling out names. Riders around the big fires put down their food, and within a few minutes, a force of thirty rhinos was rumbling off along the jungle path toward the swamp.

"Tired young Greencloaks should eat," said Xue, indicating her pot stewing over the fire. "I have a fine rat broth with bamboo shoots."

"Rat?" asked Conor.

"It tastes good," said Meilin. "Really."

"I have eaten rat," said Abeke. "Not as tasty as antelope. Can I have some, please?"

Xue smiled and bustled around, putting out bowls and spoons for everyone except Rollan, then ladling out portions of the delicious-smelling soup. Conor shared his with Briggan, but Uraza turned up her nose when Abeke offered some to the leopard.

"What about some for me?" asked Rollan plaintively.

Xue shook her head.

"No solid food till morning," she said. "Rest now."

"Just like home," said Rollan. "Never enough to eat."

But he lay back down on the grass, still wrapped in his blanket. Essix hopped off as he tilted over, and stalked across to stand near his head, a constant guardian. Rollan reached up to ruffle the falcon's feathers, a new sign of intimacy that the bird had begun to welcome.

Within a second, the boy was asleep.

"That's what I need to do," said Abeke. "But I have to get clean first. What do the riders do to wash?"

"Wait for rain," said Xue. She looked up at the dark sky. "About ten minutes."

"Might as well just . . . just lie down, then," mumbled Abeke, doing exactly that. Uraza came and stretched out next to her, paws set side by side on the ground and head placed gently upon them.

"I hope Tarik and Lishay are all right," whispered Meilin. She edged closer to Rollan, and Jhi, who was sitting next to him, apparently snoozing. But the panda shifted as Meilin sat down next to her, and put out one heavy paw to rest it across the girl's leg. The contact sent a feeling of security and comfort through her, putting all her anxieties temporarily to rest.

———◆———

The next morning did not so much dawn as gradually steam into existence. The rain kept coming down, and the sun was not strong enough to break through. Everyone woke cramped, uncomfortable, and wet. The riders had kept the big fires going all night, despite the rain, but as Meilin soon discovered, there wasn't much point trying to dry out next to them. One side would get less damp, while the other was as drenched as ever.

Breakfast came from the riders, who offered small cakes of rice mixed with some kind of mushroom. After they had eaten and sorted themselves out for the day, the Greencloaks gathered together at the rock to discuss what they should do. In the absence of Tarik, everyone looked to Xue, but the old woman refused to talk.

"I'm on holiday from the Greencloaks," she said, taking up her pack and disappearing into the outer circle of rhino riders. "Got to sell some pots."

"We should go and find Tarik and Lishay," said Abeke.

Meilin shook her head, even though her fears regarding the elder Greencloaks had returned on waking.

"We should go to Dinesh right away and convince him to give us his talisman," she said. "The Conquerors are already in the swamp, and there are a lot more of them cutting a way through the Great Bamboo Maze to the north, where I left my father. We might only be a few days ahead of them."

"Meilin's right," said Rollan. He was much better. The rash was completely gone, though he still looked weak.

"Sure, but perhaps we should try to find Tarik and Lishay first," said Conor.

"Jodoboda sent riders to look for them," said Meilin. "They would want us to go on."

"Where are we going to, exactly?" asked Conor. "Has anyone spoken to Jodoboda this morning?" He and the others looked around for him, craning their necks.

"There he is," said Rollan. "Over near that fire."

They moved as a group through the camp. Jodoboda

turned to face them as they approached.

"Our guests are anxious to depart, I see," he said.

"We need to get to Dinesh before the Conquerors," said Meilin. "But have your riders found Tarik and Lishay?"

"We will soon know."

Jodoboda held out his hand and gestured toward the jungle trail. A line of rhino riders was coming into the clearing. Several of the rhinos were riderless and had bodies strapped across their backs. Dead bodies. Jodoboda's beard quivered as the muscles of his jaw tensed. His eyes narrowed in anger.

For a moment all the Greencloaks held their breath. But at the end of the line of rhinos two familiar figures were walking together, an otter on the man's shoulder and a tiger at the woman's side. Meilin felt a surge of relief.

"Together, your friends and mine have fought many poisoned crocodiles, such as those you spoke of last night," said Jodoboda, quickly taking the measure of the situation. "The Conquerors will regret the day they brought this Bile into our lands!"

"You mean you'll fight with us against them?" asked Meilin, wondering if she could convince him to send reinforcements to her father as well.

Jodoboda shook his head, disappointing her.

"We fight alone, as we have always done. But we will not let the Conquerors trespass."

"Do you fight alone, yourself, when confronted by a foe too strong?" asked Xue, appearing from behind a crowd of rhino riders who were all holding new frying pans. "Or do you call on your riders?"

Jodoboda laughed.

"You never give up, do you? You know our traditions are as solid as the rhino rock."

Xue sniffed and muttered, "Hidebound."

Tarik and Lishay hurried over as the leader of the rhino rider patrol rode up and began talking quickly to Jodoboda.

"Rollan!" said Tarik. He looked muddy but unharmed. Lishay had a bloodstained bandage tied around her upper arm. "You look better! I knew that Abeke and Conor could get the banana gourds."

Tarik saw Xue and gawped for a moment, then bowed.

"You must be Xue," he said. "I am Tarik."

"And I, Lishay. It is an honor to meet a famous Greencloak of . . . uh . . ."

"The past?" asked Xue.

"I was going to say of 'your reputation,'" said Lishay.

"Are you joining us?" asked Tarik. "We could use your wisdom and advice."

"Not just yet," said Xue. "I still have pots to sell to some folk up north."

"Oh," said Tarik, obviously disappointed. He turned to Jodoboda. "The riders tell me that they will take us to the Lake of the Elephant. We must go now. Jodoboda, how far is it?"

"Less than a day's ride," said Jodoboda. "I will send a patrol, and you will ride with them. But tell me, where are the poisoned crocodiles and the Conquerors now?"

"All over the swamp, I hope," said Tarik. "We led them in many different directions, splitting them up and attacking the smaller groups. . . . They even attacked each other once, last night. But they will gather again, and there are other mad animals, not just the crocodiles. Whatever this poison is—"

"Abeke thinks it's the Bile," Conor offered. "The substance Zerif mentioned that gives the Conquerors their spirit animals."

Abeke nodded. "When I was with the Conquerors, I saw them transforming innocent animals with it."

"You've seen what the Conquerors will do," said Xue. "All the free peoples are needed to stop them."

"And the talismans of the Great Beasts," said Tarik. "I fear that the Conquerors may already be at the Lake of the Elephant."

"The way there is hidden," said Jodoboda. "They will not find it. Come, eat food, and clean and dress your wounds. The patrol will leave as soon as you are ready."

"We're really going to ride rhinos?" asked Conor excitedly.

"You say that as though it's a good thing," said Rollan with a worried look. Meilin, remembering how bad he was at riding horses, was unable to suppress a laugh.

17

LAKE OF THE ELEPHANT

THE WAY INTO THE LAKE OF THE ELEPHANT WAS WELL hidden. The rhino riders took the Greencloaks from the clearing along a path that gradually rose up a lengthy ridge, the jungle getting denser the higher they went. Eventually the path became more of a green tunnel, with the trees growing completely over the top and stitching themselves together with vines.

Rollan wasn't enjoying the ride. The rhinos, although smaller than their Niloan counterparts, were still very broad, and the Tergesh didn't use saddles themselves. For their passengers they had simply tied a rope around the rhino's middle. Rollan was holding on to his rope with one hand and the rider with the other, and simultaneously trying to grip the rough hide with his legs, but it was very difficult. He was feeling much better, but it still took all his energy to stay on. Several times his rider asked politely for him to stop clinging so tightly.

"I'm only holding on so tight because I'm worried your rhino will be embarrassed if I fall off," said Rollan.

The others seemed to be enjoying it. Conor whooped every time his rhino lumbered over a fallen log, and Abeke had even been allowed to swap places with her rider, to hold the chain that guided her rhino along the path.

Only Meilin rode silently. Rollan wondered if she was displaying less enthusiasm than the others in order to make him feel better.

The climb up the ridge seemed to take forever, but eventually they began to descend again, and Rollan stopped fearing that he would slip off into the mud. Halfway down, the lead rider took an even more overgrown side path, which was only just wide enough for the rhinos to pass between the ancient, massive trees. The ground became rockier, less muddy and wet, and there were fewer ferns and vines.

Another mile or so farther on, the path approached a rock face. The lead rhino reached it and disappeared. Rollan, who was on the next rhino, gasped and craned over the shoulder of his rider, wondering why they were still pressing on. Had the lead rider fallen into a hole?

Then he saw that there were actually two lines of cliff, one shielding the other. The lead rhino had turned into the narrow path between the two cliff faces, a path that led steeply down into dark shadows.

"How far's the lake now?" Rollan asked his rhino rider. "Are we almost there?"

"The lake lies ahead, still some distance."

That was what the rider always said.

"And will you wash the rhinos when you get there?" he asked, unable to resist a little dig in response.

"Rhinos do not bathe," said the rider. "Their scent sets fear in the hearts of our enemies."

"I bet." Rollan screwed up his nose.

It was very dark on the steep path downward. The trail was little more than ten feet wide between the two rock faces, and the rocky walls were at least two hundred feet high. The sun shone overhead, but little of the light made its way down to the canyon floor.

The path descended for some time, but then started to climb again. The rhinos snorted as they labored up the trail, which became steeper and steeper. Their powerful muscles flexed without any sign of fatigue. But even as the path rose up, so did the cliffsides, stretching higher still.

After several hours, Rollan thought they must have climbed at least two thousand feet. There was still no sign the path would eventually lift them out of the crack between the cliffs. At least the air had become a little less warm and humid, a welcome change after the steam of the jungle.

Finally the path began to widen out, or rather the cliffs on either side drew back. The rhinos spread out to march in pairs, side by side, and then four abreast, and finally all eight rhinos extended out into a line.

At that point, the cliff walls on either side suddenly began to grow smaller, and in the space of a few hundred yards they dwindled to nothing. The ground opened up to reveal a lake ahead, a vast pool of beautiful blue water, not at all like the muddy swamp. The lake occupied a crater of some kind, perhaps a dormant volcano, and in the middle of it there was an island with a step pyramid of gray stone built upon it. There appeared to be a dome on the top.

The rhino riders galloped their beasts down to the lakeshore and brought them to a stop in a great cloud of blown-up sand. As it cleared, Meilin suddenly fell off her rhino. She lay on the ground, stunned for a moment, looking up at the sky. Then she slowly got to her feet and stared around her at the crater walls, the island, and the sky.

"Meilin! Are you all right?" Conor was the first to leap from his own rhino, with Abeke and Rollan close behind.

Meilin didn't answer immediately. She kept looking around, her eyes glassy. She was clearly dazed by the fall. Rollan took her shoulders and tried to sit her down, but as he did so, she suddenly stepped back and thrust her arms up and out, breaking his gentle hold.

"What're you doing?" she said, suddenly alert and in the present once more.

"Helping you," he said. "You fell off the rhino."

"*I* fell off?" asked Meilin. She shook her head slightly. "I guess I was asleep. . . ."

"Outsiders often fall off," said the rhino rider who had been carrying Meilin. "On the rare occasions we let them ride with us. Luckily you fell at the *end* of the ride."

Meilin blinked and shook her head again.

"I'll be all right," she said. "Have we arrived?"

"This is the Lake of the Elephant," said the rider. "We have brought you here as Jodoboda promised. Now we must return."

The other Greencloaks slid off the rhinos' backs, took up their packs, and waved good-bye as the rhino riders remounted and set off. Rollan hadn't enjoyed the experience of being a rhino rider, but he wished they weren't leaving so soon. He felt vulnerable on the lakeshore.

"I presume the island is where we need to go," said Lishay.

Essix flew overhead, issuing a long, falling cry as she set out to inspect the way ahead. Jhi, who had chosen to travel in the dormant state, emerged with a flare of light and looked calmly out across the lake at the central island. Briggan paced along the shore, studying it with his clear blue eyes. Zhosur and Uraza tumbled out of their dormant states and briefly played some kind of cat tag, until Zhosur grew tired of it and gave up.

Lumeo, who had ridden the whole way on Tarik's shoulder, slid down his arm and went to inspect the water. But rather than slipping into it, as he normally did when finding a pleasant stream or lake, he backtracked away, letting out a strange hissing noise.

"Lumeo?" asked Tarik. He drew his sword and warily approached the lake's edge. Before he could get within a foot of the shore, a snakehead lunged up out of the clear water, needle teeth snapping at him. With a shout, Tarik slashed at it. Two wriggling pieces fell onto the shore, which Tarik kicked back into the water. A second later, the lake boiled and frothed as dozens of other snakeheads ripped the dead one apart and ate it.

"We should have brought some of those fish traps from Xin Kao Dai," said Rollan.

"We won't be swimming across," said Lishay. "And there are no trees to cut down for a raft."

There was nothing useful at all around, as far as Rollan could see. The lake was about a mile in diameter and was completely surrounded by the rocky crater wall. The only way in was behind them, through the path that wound its deep, narrow way through the mountain.

Rollan blinked, and suddenly his vision was clearer, containing more colors than he was used to. His improved vision was coming from Essix. This was the second time it had happened in such a short period, and it was no less amazing than the first.

"There are people . . . at least I think they're people . . . on the island," said Rollan, shading his eyes and peering across the water. "They've got weird heads, way too big for their bodies. There are three of them watching us. . . . Look near the middle of the pyramid, at the bottom."

The others all looked. They too could see the three small figures, but it was too far away for them to make out who or what they were. They stood near the base of the pyramid, looking back at the Greencloaks for a while, then turned and disappeared somewhere inside the structure.

"There must be a boat or something hidden somewhere along here," said Abeke. "Over there, the crater wall looks different. . . ."

"Yes, I see it," said Tarik. About a hundred yards away, there was a stretch of the crater wall that looked smooth, as if the stone had been worked. "Let's go take a look."

It was clear the crater rim wall had been not only smoothed but also deeply carved with an intricate design. In it, an elephant wading through a river or lake raised its trunk to spray water in the air.

"Subtle," said Rollan. "I think we've definitely found the Lake of the Elephant."

"It might be more than that," said Meilin. She moved closer to the stone and ran her fingers along the carved lines. "Some of these are cut much deeper. . . . I wonder."

She stepped back to get a wider view, her eyes following the deep marks, which were darker on the stone.

"There's a door," she said. "Look, follow the deep lines. They go up that leg, across the body, down the back leg, and then along the lake. And there's a line in the middle as well. It's a rectangle cut in the middle. Double doors!"

"Maybe," said Conor, scratching his head. "Tight-fitting doors, if they are. How do you get them open?"

"I don't know that," replied Meilin. "Yet."

"Secret doors are often activated by pushing or pulling something," said Tarik. "Well-spotted, Meilin."

"What about its eye?" said Conor. "That sticks out a lot more than anything else. We could try to push it in."

"I could jump up and kick it," said Abeke.

"Wait!" said Rollan. "There might be a trap. Maybe the eye is too obvious. We should try and poke it with a stick from the side, not from in front."

"I could do that with my staff," said Meilin. "If I stand over here . . ."

"Everyone, get well back," said Tarik.

Meilin waited until they were all clear, then climbed up near the elephant carving. She leaned across and extended her staff as far as she could, until it pressed against the eye. It moved, depressing several inches.

There was a loud click and a dozen arrows shot out from holes disguised in the carving. If Abeke had jumped to kick the eyeball, she would have been hit for sure.

"I guess Dinesh really doesn't want visitors," said Rollan.

"If it's not the eye, then what else could trigger it to open?" mused Abeke. She walked in front of the door and looked again.

But nothing else was immediately obvious, not until Lumeo suddenly straightened up on Tarik's shoulder and chittered something in his ear.

"Of course," said Tarik. He pointed to a tiny carving, smaller than his thumb, in the water the elephant was standing in, just near its tail. "A boat!"

"Looks more like a banana gourd," said Rollan. "Or a squashed insect."

"Those are oars, not legs," said Conor. "It is a boat."

"I can probably press it from the other side," said Meilin.

She scrambled up the crater wall on the right-hand side of the carving. Rollan went with her, while everyone else retreated to what they hoped were safe positions.

The staff was extended. It was a long reach, and the staff was heavy. Despite her best efforts and Rollan's encouragement, Meilin couldn't stop the end from waving around so much that she couldn't touch the tiny boat.

"Jhi!" she called. "Come and help me!"

The panda ambled over and sat down below Meilin. Meilin took a deep breath in and out, and grew still all over. Rollan had never seen her look so . . . not relaxed, but rather composed, as though all the drive and urgency had left her for a moment, leaving her at a still point he could only envy.

With perfect focus, Meilin reached out once more with

her staff. It was steady in her hands and she guided it exactly onto the tiny carving of the boat.

A deep rumbling sounded inside the crater wall. Dust fell from the elephant carving, and the two halves of the door slowly lowered forward, like a drawbridge opening.

"Wait!" cautioned Tarik as Conor moved to go inside.

A forty-foot-long boat came rolling out, propelled by hidden mechanisms within the cave. It was made of tightly woven reeds, with its long mast lying flat along its length and oars shipped, mounted on a carriage that ran across the lowered bridge toward the lake.

Rollan dropped down the crater wall and ran after it, grabbing at the ropes that trailed behind to bring it to a stop before it hit the water and drifted off without them.

18

THE ISLAND PYRAMID

ONCE ROLLAN HAD CAUGHT THE BOAT AND THE OTHERS had helped pull it back up the shore, it was easy to get it in the water and climb aboard. Everyone was very careful to climb in over the stern and not step into the water, which made it a little difficult to push the craft off the shore. Once on the lake, the lightness of its construction and lack of a keel also meant the boat was easily caught by the wind, so it needed four of them rowing all the time just to keep it going roughly toward the island. As the oars dipped in and out of the water, snakeheads snapped at them.

"There is a strong current," said Tarik, who was managing the steering oar. He looked around the crater rim. "There must be a river coming in somewhere."

"There," said Rollan, pointing. He was acting as a lookout in the bow, while the others rowed. There was a patch of darkness low on the northern crater wall. Essix, on his shoulder, shrieked in confirmation.

"Another way in," said Tarik thoughtfully. "For things like crocodiles."

"At least we got here first," said Meilin.

"Maybe we can get the talisman and be gone before Zerif and the Conquerors even work out where we are," said Conor.

"Their seer is very powerful," said Abeke, looking around her. "Getting in and out unhindered might be too much to hope for."

"Uh, those big-headed people are coming out of the pyramid again," said Rollan, sounding as nervous as Abeke felt. "Oh, they've got elephant heads! Wait, that can't be right. . . ."

"Don't stop rowing!" called Tarik as everyone turned around to look. "They're just masks."

"Um, they've got bows," said Rollan. "We'll be in range very soon."

"Abeke, Lishay, take up your bows," said Tarik.

"I only have three arrows left," said Abeke. "One of them is bent."

"I have five," said Lishay.

"There are twenty of the elephant heads," said Rollan. "They've all got bows. . . . *They're nocking arrows!*"

"Rowers, backwater!" said Tarik. "We'll try to parley with them. Rollan, take the steering oar."

Tarik and Rollan swapped ends, Tarik putting one foot up on the boat's elephant figurehead, one of the only wooden parts of the reed ship. He cupped his hands around his mouth and shouted.

"We are Greencloaks, come to visit Dinesh!"

One of the elephant heads took off a mask, revealing a

middle-aged woman with gray-painted skin.

"The elephant does not want visitors! Turn back!"

"We must see Dinesh!" shouted Tarik. "It is of vital importance!"

"Turn back!" shouted the woman. "We will shoot!"

"If you shoot, we must fight you!" roared Tarik. "We don't want that. We are Greencloaks, we are Marked, and we have spirit animals! You will all be killed."

"Turn back!"

"No! We must talk to Dinesh!"

The woman put her elephant head back on and lowered her arm. Immediately, the others fired, arrows arcing toward the boat.

"Backwater!" ordered Tarik. He stood where he was, watching the flight of the arrows. When they reached the peak of their trajectory, he drew his sword, ready to cut the projectiles from the air. But he didn't need to, as they fell short.

"Abeke, shoot at the one who spoke," said Tarik. "Aim for the legs. . . . We don't want to kill anyone unnecessarily."

Abeke and Lishay stood by the rail, bending their knees to compensate for the slight roll of the boat.

"Left leg for me," said Lishay. "Below the knee."

"I'll try for her right," said Abeke, aiming carefully.

They shot at the same time, their arrows flying in a much flatter arc than the elephant-head arrows. A loud scream announced they had hit something, and a moment later the spokeswoman fell to the ground. Four other elephant heads hastily dropped their bows and picked her up, carrying her inside the pyramid.

"And then there were fifteen," said Conor.

Tarik cupped his hands and shouted again. "We don't want to fight you! Let us land and speak to Dinesh!"

The only answer was another shower of arrows. Tarik chopped two of them out of the air, and Meilin deflected another with her quarterstaff.

"Shoot two more in the legs," sighed Tarik. "If only they had some sense!"

"They don't know who we are," said Meilin. "They probably think we're the Conquerors."

"A half-dozen people in a raft?" said Rollan. "Though I suppose we could be scouts. . . ."

Abeke and Lishay shot again. This time, six people helped each of the wounded inside, leaving only three archers behind. They bravely stood their ground, until Lishay and Abeke began to draw their bowstrings back. Then they made the sensible decision to retreat inside before any more arrows could be loosed in their direction.

"Quickly, row in before they come back with reinforcements," said Tarik.

"Their range is short because their bows are inferior," said Lishay. "Do not assume that these are their only weapons."

"All we have to do is talk to them," said Abeke. She hadn't liked firing at people who couldn't hit her back. "I am sure they will see reason."

"Who are they?" asked Conor.

"Priests, I would guess," said Tarik. "Serving Dinesh as a divine being. It has happened often with the Great Beasts, although they don't encourage it, usually."

There was a wooden quay on the island, in front

of the pyramid. They moored the boat there and went ashore cautiously, weapons ready. But no elephant heads remained in view, and the huge bronze doors at the foot of the pyramid were firmly closed.

Rollan sent Essix to fly around and see if there was another way in, while Tarik knocked firmly on the huge door.

"We are Greencloaks," he called out, "here to see Dinesh! We mean no harm!"

There was no answer, and the huge doors did not open.

"Didn't we just shoot three of them?" said Rollan. "No wonder they don't want to talk to . . . uh, wait."

Essix had swooped back and circled once over his head, before taking off again.

"Something about the top of the pyramid," said Rollan. "I think maybe Essix has found another way in!"

"Well done." Tarik started to climb up, followed by Meilin, Abeke, Rollan, and Conor, with Lishay at the rear, all but Rollan with their spirit animals dormant. The pyramid was built in a series of steps or tiers, each one about four feet high. It was difficult, but not impossible, for Abeke to haul herself up onto the next level. There were thirty-nine steps, Abeke calculated. Not too many to wear Rollan out in his recovering state, she hoped. On the fourth step he faltered, and Conor reached down a hand to help him. Rollan took it, nodding in gratitude.

Tarik was on the fifteenth step when he stopped for a rest and looked out across the lake.

"Look! Over there!"

There were dark shapes in the clear waters of the lake, coming out at the spot where the underground river flowed in. Dozens and dozens of them, massive things under the water.

"Crocodiles!" said Abeke. "The Conquerors must be using them to attack! But surely the snakeheads will—"

She faltered, seeing sudden flurries in the water. Smaller darting shapes were attacking the larger ones, sending up a frothy spray tinged with pink. But they didn't last long. The crocodiles could kill several snakeheads with one snap of their jaws, and the sharp teeth of the carnivorous fish had trouble penetrating the crocs' armored hides. A few of the smaller ones floated dead to the surface, but plenty more snakeheads kept on coming, pushing through the mashed-up remains of hundreds of others. It was telling that the crocs were so affected by the Bile that they didn't stop to eat the dead fish.

"There are people on the crater wall," said Rollan. "Soldiers."

"And spirit animals!" said Conor, shielding his eyes. "It looks like the Conquerors."

Abeke could just make out lines of soldiers who were throwing ropes down the sides of the inner crater wall. "But how did they find this place?"

Meilin shook her head.

"I don't know. I think they're the same ones I saw attacking my father, but to get here so quickly . . . They must have come the same way I did, through the Maze!"

"I hope Essix really has found a way into the temple," said Tarik grimly. "Come on!"

They raced to the top now, helping each other up. But when at last they reached the summit and the base of the dome they found there, there was no obvious door. Just the dome, which appeared to be one huge boulder of pitted gray stone, much, much larger than any of the blocks that had built the rest of the pyramid. It towered over them, covered with strange sweeping marks and lines, almost like a map of the world.

"Are you pulling our legs, Essix?" chided Rollan. "If the entrance is *under* that thing, we're never going to—"

Essix's retort was indignant from where she circled the dome above them.

"I don't get it," said Rollan to the others, looking apologetic on behalf of his spirit animal. "I'm sure she's telling us that the way in is right here, somewhere."

"We need to find it soon," said Meilin. "Those crocs are halfway across the lake, and they're big enough to climb up here!"

"Maybe Briggan can find a way," said Conor. He called the wolf, who appeared in a flash of light. He immediately went to the huge boulder, sniffed it, and sat down.

"Briggan says it's here too," said Conor, mystified. "I mean, that's not it exactly, it's more a kind of sense of having arrived where we wanted to go. . . ."

He moved back from the dome and looked at it speculatively. Rollan joined him, Essix still calling out what sounded like falcon for bad words above his head. Abeke called Uraza, who looked up at her in puzzlement, as though not understanding why the humans couldn't see something obvious.

"So show us," Abeke said. "What are we missing?"

Uraza loped forward until she was directly in front of the dome. Raising both front paws, she raked her claws down the side of the stone. Sparks danced from the stone, and a faint curl of what looked like smoke.

There came a great rumble that shook the entire pyramid, and a flurry of movement as everyone jumped, dropped, or half fell onto the next step down. Uraza backed hastily away, and looked up expectantly.

Another booby trap, thought Abeke. What if the dome were to collapse, destroying the temple they were standing on? She scrambled backward so quickly she fell over. When she tried to stand, Uraza coiled through her legs, making her fall over again.

She stared upward in horror, then amazement, as the huge boulder slowly rose above her and began to uncurl, the mysterious lines in its stone flank widening and becoming the gap between limbs and an enormous body. First there was a questing trunk, as long as the trunk of the mightiest tree in the jungle, then one massive foot, and then another, planting themselves firmly on the highest step of the pyramid, and *lifting*.

Suddenly a massive elephant was standing above them, making everything below seem small.

With thundering steps, it shifted position so its fierce eyes could look down on the Greencloaks from above. Tusks that were easily twelve yards long and looked very sharp swayed from side to side, hissing through the air.

"What do I have to do to be left alone?!" roared Dinesh the Elephant.

19

DINESH

MEILIN WAS THE FIRST TO FIND HER VOICE. ROLLAN'S throat was closed tight, not just by the dust Dinesh's appearance had raised, but by the fear of being crushed under one of those terrible feet. Or skewered on a tusk . . . or swept in by that mighty trunk and swallowed whole.

"We do not disturb your rest lightly," Meilin said with a deep bow. "The crocodiles are creatures poisoned by the Conquerors, who serve the new Devourer. We are ambassadors from the Greencloaks, companions of the Four Fallen, and we need your help!"

With that, she released Jhi onto the step beside her. Leopard and wolf loped to join the panda, while falcon swooped low overhead, and then screeched away.

Dinesh leaned down, an unnerving action given his enormous size. The pyramid groaned under his weight. Rollan was sure he felt the stones shifting beneath his feet.

"Yes, I see Jhi is your companion; and there is Uraza, who woke me from my quiet contemplation; and Essix,

152

aloof as ever; and Briggan, wanting to bite someone, no doubt. . . . I have not missed them. They are small, but I suppose they might grow."

"Time is short, Dinesh," said Tarik. "We are beset upon by not only crocodiles but also an army, with many spirit animals. They will take rather than talk."

"Take? Take what?"

"Your talisman, Dinesh," said Rollan, finding his voice. "The Slate Elephant."

"I see," rumbled Dinesh. "That would not be easily taken. It is what you have also come for, is it not?"

"It is," said Abeke. "We need it, to fight the Devourer."

"You say the Devourer has also come again?" asked Dinesh. "Are Kovo and Gerathon released from their prisons?"

"We do not know," said Tarik. "But the enemy has over-run many lands, and agents of the Devourer seek all the talismans. They have the Iron Boar already."

"And you have the Granite Ram," said Dinesh, his eyes bright on Abeke, as if he could sense the talisman on her.

"We need your talisman desperately," said Conor. "If you give it to us, we might still be able to —"

"Get away from these crocodiles and soldiers?" asked Dinesh.

"Use it to fight them," said Abeke.

"Ah, I misjudged you," said Dinesh. The huge elephant sighed and looked out at the approaching crocodiles and the northern crater wall, which was now swarming with soldiers. There were rope ladders all along the crater rim, and many ropes. There were also boats being lowered: long, light canoes that must have been carried for miles through the Great Bamboo Maze, and then the jungle.

"Will you give us your talisman?" asked Conor quietly.

The elephant shifted with a sound of rock grinding against rock.

"It is no small thing you ask," he said. "The Great Beasts and our talismans, we are two sides of one thing, fruit of the same tree. . . . To give up our talismans is to give up something of ourselves. But then I suppose we must all face the time for change, when it comes, in our different ways. Even when we try to escape it, like Suka in her tomb of ice. Though in her case, I am not sure avoidance was her intention."

"Suka the Polar Bear?" asked Tarik. "She is entombed in ice?"

"Yes. At least, that was the last I heard of her. I have not kept up with my fellows. I have not kept up with the world."

"Now the world is coming to you, whether you like it or not," said Rollan. "In about five minutes, there are going to be hundreds of those Bile creatures swarming up here, and an army of enemies not long after that. So are you going to give us the Slate Elephant or not?"

"I will let fate choose for me," mused Dinesh. "Let us see who is alive by the end of the day. But I am inclined to help you at least a little. I will tell the people who have decided to be my priests to fight with you, to make it a little less one-sided."

The massive elephant stood up on his hind legs, an incredible sight. He lifted his trunk and trumpeted a call that echoed across the crater, and probably for miles beyond. Then he curled up again at the top of the pyramid, his skin darkening and turning to stone, and once more became a giant impenetrable dome.

But his trumpet call still echoed around the crater, or so it seemed, until the listeners realized they were hearing answering calls as well. Faint horn blasts came from the narrow path between the cliffs, accompanied by the clash of Zhongese gongs.

But the Greencloaks had no time to wonder what this meant. They were jumping down the pyramid, running for the great bronze gate even as the first of the Bile-grown crocodiles came sliding ashore.

Rollan lagged slightly behind, still feeling winded from the ascent. He could see three waves converging on the same spot: him and the others, with their spirit animals; the crocodiles, whipping through the water with powerful swishes of their Bile-fueled tails; and Dinesh's priests. He worried that the crocodiles would reach the gate before anyone else, but it was the Greencloaks who got there first, turning at the last moment to face their enemies. Tarik's and Lishay's spirit animals exploded out to join them, ready for combat.

Dinesh's priests rushed forward to stand at their sides. The priests were now clad in chain mail. Their bulbous paper elephant heads had been replaced by sleek steel helmets with thin, daggerlike tusks. They carried long spears and swords, and pointed knives hung from their belts. With a series of brisk commands, they arrayed themselves in front of the gates, smoothly assimilating the Greencloaks into their defensive wall.

The first wave of crocodiles struck in a fury of muscle and teeth. Most went down quickly: spitted on spears, stabbed by Tarik's sword, and shot with elephant priests' arrows snatched up by Abeke and Lishay. Those that got through were chopped with Conor's ax, bitten by Briggan, and stabbed in the eyes by Rollan. Uraza and Zhosur prowled the fringes of the battle, savaging anything that survived.

Despite this, one particularly large croc almost managed to get past the defenders, only to be distracted by Lumeo, snapping after the otter so wildly it almost tied itself in a knot. As it tried to disentangle its tail from its legs, Conor's ax came down on its head.

The second wave was only minutes behind, but it gave Tarik a brief time to organize the defenses.

"Shut the gates!" he commanded, throwing himself against one of the massive bronze doors. It slowly groaned forward, until he was joined by half a dozen elephant priests who pushed it swiftly closed. Clanging shut, huge locking bars automatically fell into position.

"Are there arrow ports?" asked Tarik.

"Yes," said a tall priest, sliding back several panels at chest height.

"Lishay, Abeke, shoot through those," said Tarik. He looked around the huge central chamber. There were at least forty armed and armored elephant priests there, but another dozen or so were still in their gray robes, gathered around a huge bronze wheel that stuck out of the far wall.

"What's that wheel?"

"It opens the water gate," said one of the unhelmeted priests. He looked younger than most of the others, and seemed more alert, less confused by the sudden change in what must have been a quiet and orderly existence up until that day. "To drain the lake."

"How quickly does it do that?" asked Tarik.

"We do not know," said the priest. "It's a defense of last resort. It has never been done before."

"If it's fast enough, it will take the enemy's boats away," said Conor. "Suck them under!"

Tarik nodded. "Is there anywhere to see out from above? We need to know if the Conquerors have launched their boats."

The priest pointed to a stairway on the left.

"There are disguised viewing ports at every step," he said. "But once opened, they might be spotted from outside."

"Rollan, go see what the enemy is doing," said Tarik.

Rollan hurried up the stairs as the bronze doors rang out with the sudden impact of massive crocodiles throwing themselves against the gate. Conor came with him. Abeke and Lishay began to shoot steadily through the arrow ports, taking careful aim with each shot. Without being asked, elephant priests brought them quivers full of new arrows.

Rollan was panting by the time he reached the fourth level. Conor joined him at the viewing port, and together they squinted out across the lake.

Neither of them needed Essix's falcon sight to take stock of the forces arrayed below.

"They're on the lake!" Conor called back down, since Rollan was still breathless. "And there's a huge – I mean really huge – crocodile driving the other ones ahead of it!"

"The Devourer himself must be here," they heard Tarik say. Someone gasped.

"If we could defeat him . . ." said Conor. "That might finish the war right here!"

Rollan blinked at his friend. It seemed to him a bit optimistic, when they were outnumbered a thousand to one, with a truly giant crocodile on the warpath and who knew what other Bile-created spirit animals.

They hurried back down the steps to ground level, where the very same conversation was taking place.

"Did you see anyone coming through the cliff path?" Meilin asked Rollan and Conor. "Rhino riders or Zhongese forces?"

"No," said Rollan, panting. "Just thousands and thousands of Conquerors, swarming over the crater wall, with hundreds of boats."

"Are there many on the water already?" asked Tarik.

"A third, maybe more," said Conor.

"Open the water gate!" commanded Tarik.

The priests at the huge bronze wheel gripped it and tried to turn it, some pulling and some pushing. But it refused to budge.

The gate rang out again, the bars groaning as they held against another attack by enraged crocodiles.

"They're throwing themselves at the gate in a frenzy. They're totally mad!" shouted Abeke, taking up another arrow and firing it. "I've shot this one a dozen times, and it's still attacking!"

"Everyone but Abeke and Lishay to the wheel!" ordered Tarik. "You priests, stand back!"

Conor and Briggan, Rollan and Essix, Meilin and Jhi,

and Tarik and Lumeo raced over to the huge wheel.

"Take hold, and call upon the strength of your spirit animal!" said Tarik.

Everyone heaved, but the wheel still wouldn't budge. Behind them, the huge doors rang again as the crocodiles rammed into it, this time with an alarming cracking sound from the bars that held it closed.

"The gate's breaking!" shouted Lishay.

"Heave!"

The wheel still did not move.

"Jhi! Help me!" called out Meilin.

Jhi lumbered up onto her hind legs and ponderously approached the wheel, laying her paws down on one of the thick spokes. Rollan had heard about the strength the panda had displayed in the Great Bamboo Maze, but he had never seen it in action.

"Everyone, *now*!" called out Meilin. Rollan shut his eyes and pushed against the wheel with all his strength, as everyone around him exerted every scrap of muscle and determination.

There was a sound like gravel crunching as the rust that had locked the wheel in place disintegrated. It started to move, slowly at first, and then more swiftly, until it was spinning almost of its own accord.

"Rollan, go and see if this has done anything!" ordered Tarik. As he spoke, one of the bars that held the gate splintered and broke, leaving only one beam of wood holding the doors shut. "Everyone else, prepare to receive the enemy!"

Abeke and Lishay jumped aside as the last bar snapped. A hideous, red-eyed crocodile charged through the gap, and was immediately set upon by elephant priests with their spears. More crocs came behind, sending the bronze doors crashing open. They were met by a charge from Tarik and the others. The inside of the pyramid was a vicious battle with everyone screaming, and crocs smashing into stone in their frenzy.

Rollan ran back up the stairs, calling Essix's name. He didn't stop to look out through any of the lower view ports, racing up to the eighth step, which he knew would give an even better view over the lake. Hastily sliding it open, he looked out.

The enemy armada was halfway across the lake, heading toward the island. Hundreds of canoe-like boats were already on the water, with at least as many being launched.

He couldn't see the giant crocodile, though, which was alarming. And there didn't appear to be anything happening to the lake, at least not on the northern side.

Rollan shut the port and ran around the walkway to the eastern side. He looked out. Their only chance was if a strong enough current sucked the boats down and took the soldiers and their spirit animals with them.

Again, there was nothing. Rollan ran to the southern side. Essix screeched above his head and plummeted down into view, landing several feet short of the view port. Rollan felt a now-familiar rush of falcon sight that brought him too many details of the approaching horde, but still no sign of the Devourer.

There was something else, though. Something on the pyramid at Essix's feet, just outside the viewing port. The stone there was a slightly different color from all the other blocks that made up the pyramid. It was a darker gray, actually closer to the real color of Dinesh than the rest of the pyramid, and there was something carved on the surface.

Rollan reached through the viewing port and brushed the stone, Essix closely watching his every move. There was a small elephant the size of his palm carved into the gray stone. He traced it with his finger and, perhaps with too much daring, pushed against it.

The carving popped out. There was a small gray elephant with a golden chain connected to its back.

It was the Slate Elephant. The talisman!

Rollan's hand closed to pick it up, his thoughts racing. Now that they had it, they could try to escape, take the reed boat and run for the path through the cliff. They might make it . . . though it would be incredibly risky, even with the talisman.

Dinesh's talisman. He hadn't given it to them. Rollan had found it. Taking it now would be stealing, and did Rollan really want a giant angry elephant coming after him to get it back?

He had stolen things in Concorba; he'd had to simply in order to survive. But he didn't think of himself as a thief. He'd had a code that had stopped him going down a path that led many orphans just like him to becoming hardened criminals, or worse. *Never take from the poor, never from the sick, and never if there was a better way.* Didn't that apply here too? Wouldn't it be better to earn it rather than take it?

His fingers itched. Dinesh was so powerful. Imagine what his talisman could do!

Slowly, not at all certain he wasn't being a complete

idiot, not daring to imagine what Meilin might say if she found out, Rollan pushed the tiny elephant back in place.

As it locked home, he heard a voice in his head.

Good, said Dinesh. *If you had taken the talisman against my will, you would be my enemy. Since you have given it back, I will be your friend.*

Essix nodded approvingly and Rollan sagged in relief.

"Uh, thanks," said Rollan, though he wasn't sure if Dinesh could hear him or if this mental speech only went one way. "How about being real friendly and helping us *right now*?"

There was no response. Essix launched into air and flew to the next port. He ran after her and threw the cover open.

Looking out, this time he was rewarded with a much better view. A circular hole had opened in the southern crater wall, a hole he estimated to be about fifty feet in diameter, though most of it was underwater. Water roiled and frothed near it, and a whirlpool was forming, showing that the lake was emptying out. But it wasn't emptying *fast* enough. The current wouldn't be strong enough to sweep the invading army away.

Help is coming, said Dinesh. *Look to the west.*

20

LAST STAND

CONOR STEPPED BACK FROM THE BATTLEGROUND, WIPING his ax on his tunic as he recovered his breath. The crocodiles in the first two waves had all been killed. Greencloaks and elephant priests stood somberly among the carnage, checking weapons and wounds. Meilin helped bandage a badly bitten priest, with Jhi gently licking at the wound.

"We cannot hold here with the gates broken like this," said Tarik to Lishay, who was cleaning some recovered arrows. "We will have to make a stand on the pyramid above, or run for the boat, if the lake is not emptying too fast."

"We can't all fit on the boat," said Conor with a worried glance at the priests. After their awkward start approaching the island, they had fought well together. The priests didn't deserve to be left behind.

But if they *didn't* take the boat, they might all die here. The Conquerors would win, and the world of Erdas would be lost to the Devourer.

Rollan came racing down the stairs, completely winded.

"The lake *is* emptying," he panted. "But not fast enough. Enemy boats are halfway across—" He paused to suck in a breath. "But there is good news. Rhino riders are coming down the cliff path! And there are Zhongese soldiers too, under silver and crimson banners!"

"Silver and crimson!" exclaimed Meilin. "My father!"

"I cannot think what would have brought them," said Tarik. "But now we have a chance."

"Xue," said Conor. "I'll bet she called them."

"Did you see the Devourer?" asked Tarik. "Or his giant crocodile?"

Rollan shook his head.

"How far away are the boats?"

"About ten minutes," said Rollan. "But some were already turning aside to go back to shore, to prepare for the rhino riders' attack."

"We'd better go and have a look," said Tarik. "Stay close and be ready to retreat back here."

"Essix . . . says that the way is clear," said Rollan, his gaze turning distant. "If we go out now, we won't be surprised by that giant croc."

Conor glanced at Briggan, who was standing over a dead crocodile as though daring it to wake up, and smiled contentedly. Even if they did die in battle today, he had experienced more than he had ever dreamed of while herding sheep.

Tarik wiped his sword on his trouser leg. The others formed up behind him in a wedge. Zhosur and Uraza pounced ahead, one to either side, with Briggan stalking out in front. Jhi gave the wounded priest one last lick and entered the dormant state as a tattoo on Meilin's arm.

Together, they walked out into the sunshine, past the broken gates and the crocodiles outside, whose heads were stuck with so many arrows they looked like bizarre oversized pincushions. Essix swooped low overhead with a shriek that made the priests start.

The great host of the Conquerors was still pouring over the crater wall, thousands of them, and it seemed nearly all had spirit animals. There were lynxes and cougars, jackals and boars, bears and hyenas – all kinds of animals swarming ahead of the soldiers. In the air above, there were bats and ravens, vultures and hawks.

The lake was filling up with boats, although none had made it to the center yet. The lake was also clearly shallower, the mark of its former level visible along the shore. But even though it was emptying, the current only sped the attackers' boats faster toward the island.

On the western shore, the Conquerors were forming up in ranks. A mile south, rhino riders swarmed from the cliff path, each one dropping a Zhongese soldier from its back as they came out, the crimson lacquer on their armor bright as they ran into their tight formations.

But even rhino riders and Zhongese together were greatly outnumbered by the Conquerors.

"They'll be overwhelmed," said Meilin softly, looking at the Zhongese. Conor wondered if she was remembering the fall of Jano Rion. "We all will be. There are just too many of them."

Conor's heart sank. She was right. The hope that they had felt at the news of the arrival of the rhino riders and the Zhongese soldiers was ebbing away.

"If you're going to help us," said Rollan beside him, "now would be a very good time."

Conor turned to stare at his friend in puzzlement. Rollan was looking away from the host, not toward it.

"Who're you talking to?" Conor asked him.

"Uh . . . Dinesh. He owes me. I think. Or maybe he was just—"

Rollan gripped Conor's shoulder as the island suddenly jolted beneath them.

"What was that?" Conor looked down at the ground. It felt like an earthquake.

"Look!" Rollan was pointing up at the dome. It seemed to be rising higher above the top of the pyramid, as though Dinesh was stirring again.

Then Conor saw that the massive blocks in front of the dome were being pushed aside, as though the dome were the top of a giant sphere . . . a sphere that was starting to roll—

"Run!" shrieked Rollan. "Run left!"

Everyone turned around and saw the now massively unbalanced sphere. It was almost half the size of the pyramid itself and still moving forward, pushing through the stone blocks as though they were a child's bricks.

It was about to burst free and roll down the remaining steps of the pyramid onto them.

The ground shook violently as it crushed down the first step, grinding the stone into a ramp. The Greencloaks and elephant priests fled toward the edge of the island. The boulder smashed down several more steps, straightening its path, and seeming to grow bigger as it approached. It was at least a hundred feet in diameter. Conor didn't remember Dinesh being *that* big.

Halfway down the pyramid, the massive boulder bounced into the air and came crashing down with a thud that knocked everyone off their feet. Then it bounced again.

It rose high in the air, higher than any stone could normally bounce, and grew once more. Conor gaped as it soared overhead, impossibly high and huge at the same time. It was now the size of a tiny moon, a vast ball of stone that tumbled as it fell—straight at the enemy's fleet.

The boulder struck the surface of the lake with incredible force, blowing most of the remaining water out of the lake in a single titanic splash. Boats, soldiers, spirit animals, crocodiles, everything exploded up into the air before coming down again in a torrent.

Conor lay on the ground, shielding his head. He held his breath as water cascaded down all around them. A wave smashed against the island, its wash spreading all the way to the pyramid. But it was weaker than it might have been. Most of the water had gone up in the air.

Conor was the first to stand up. He looked around anxiously for Briggan, fear stabbing at his heart. Then he saw him, crouching with the big cats, teeth bared. He shook all over, sending spray everywhere. The other spirit animals were all right, even Essix. The falcon was a black speck high above.

Something flopped at Conor's feet. It was a snakehead, trying to bite him even as it gasped in the open air. He put it out of its misery with a quick stroke of his ax.

From nearby came the trumpeting cry of an elephant.

"Look!" cried Rollan, pointing.

The lake was now dry, the rocky bed exposed, covered

in wounded Conquerors and smashed boats. Right in the middle, the massive boulder that had caused the deluge uncurled, and there was Dinesh the Elephant. He raised his trunk and trumpeted another war cry, but there were no enemies nearby to attack.

Conor raised his ax above his head, but not in triumph, not yet. Things were different on the shore. The Conquerors were advancing. Even with a good third of their number lost upon the lake, it was still a great host, marching inexorably toward the smaller forces of the rhino riders and the Zhongese resistance. The rhinos were closest to what had been the lakeshore, with the Zhongese foot soldiers forming up on the lower slopes of the crater wall.

Down in the lake bed, Dinesh trumpeted again and began to lumber across toward the forthcoming battlefield. As he moved forward, there was a great blast of horns from the rhino riders. Conor saw Jodoboda raise his lance and bring it down, and all the rhino riders charged toward the enemy, the rhinos lowering their massive, horned heads.

The Greencloaks surged forward instinctively too, sprinting over the rocky bed to join in the battle.

"Wait!" said Tarik. "We must think before we fight, and stand together. Where can we make best use of our talents?"

Conor knew where Meilin wanted to go. She was anxiously appraising the force of Zhongese resistance fighters, no doubt looking for her father.

"We might get trampled by the rhinos in a fight," he said. "It would be safer for us with General Teng."

Meilin glanced at him, as though surprised to hear him suggesting that plan. Her desire to agree was naked on her face, but with a brisk shake of her head and a hint of anguish in her eyes, she said, "My father doesn't need us. Dinesh is one against many. We should follow Dinesh and protect him."

Tarik nodded. "I agree. We follow Dinesh, and stay together!"

He ran swiftly forward, Lumeo on his shoulder, lending him speed and agility over the exposed lake bed. The others followed as best they could, watching the rhinos on the other side surging into the Conquerors, who had stopped to receive their charge, shields and spears at the ready.

The clash of so many rhinos, spirit animals, and soldiers and their weapons made a sound none of the Greencloaks had ever heard before. It was like a terrible shout of pain and anger from a metallic throat, louder than anything.

A minute after the rhinos charged home, Dinesh joined the fray. Many Conquerors ran before him, both spirit animals and people, but some were made of sterner stuff. Soon he was surrounded and had to turn in a circle, trumpeting and crushing, picking up enemies with his trunk and hurling them back against their allies. His tusks cut like scythes through the Conqueror ranks, leaving wide swathes felled in their wake.

The rhino riders found themselves surrounded too. Their charge had taken them deep into the enemy forces, but there were too many Conquerors. They spread around and forward, cutting the rhino riders off from their allies, the Zhongese resistance fighters, on the crater wall.

In response to this, a blast of battle gongs sounded from the resistance fighters, and Conor made out a tall man at the front pointing his sword forward, catching the sunlight. Surely that was General Teng, giving the command to advance! Meilin's face lit up with pride, and Conor cheered as the well-disciplined Zhongese soldiers marched forward, pausing every ten yards or so to unleash a volley of arrows.

Then it was time for Tarik and the others to enter the fight. They had reached the confused melee behind Dinesh, and Conor gripped his ax tightly with both hands, preparing himself for battle. Beside him, Briggan barked and snapped at the air, eager to get his teeth into the enemy. On the other side of the wolf, Rollan grinned at him.

"Together, right?"

Conor grinned back. "Always."

The sentiment was a fine one, but as they cut their way toward the elephant, almost immediately the press of battle began to force them apart.

"Pair up!" shouted Tarik as he dodged beneath the swipe of a huge soldier with a two-handed ax and cut at his arm, Lumeo dancing around below, biting at the man's hamstrings to bring him down. As the enemy soldier fell, Zhosur jumped on him and bit him in the neck, before leaping across to savage a jackal that was trying to bite Lishay.

Conor found himself back-to-back with Abeke, surrounded by enemies. They fought together as they had in the swamp, Briggan and Uraza at their sides. Conor and the two spirit animals kept the soldiers back with his ax, while Abeke coolly shot them.

"They're faltering!" shouted Tarik. "Press on!"

The Conquerors *were* beginning to waver, and many were glancing over their shoulders. The ones between the rhino riders and the Zhongese fighters began to look for ways out, and some even started to surrender, throwing down their weapons.

The battle was on a knife-edge between defeat and victory. Anything could happen in the next few seconds. The whole future might be decided in that time. Hope suddenly rose in the hearts of the defenders as the Conquerors felt their first real pangs of fear.

Then a great crocodile, even larger than the others, came out of the lake bed.

"I've seen that one before," gasped Abeke, pulling an arrow out of the body of a Conqueror who had fallen at her feet.

Conor wiped sweat from his forehead. "Is it—?"

"Yes. I saw it curled in front of the throne of the Devourer." Her expression was very fierce.

"The Devourer," whispered Conor, and his words rang out in a sudden hush. All fighting had momentarily ceased, everyone looking at the giant crocodile in awe.

A huge man stood up on the crocodile's back. He was armored in red mail, with a fanged helmet that hid his face.

"General Gar or not, I'll put an arrow in him just the same," said Abeke.

The arrival of the crocodile and its rider put new heart in the Conquerors. A cry went up and they charged forward again. The battle swirled and shifted, small groups fighting in all directions, all order crumbling into chaos.

Conor had lost sight of the other Greencloaks. He stayed close to Abeke. They fell into a rhythm that was only broken when a wolverine attacked Conor from behind while he was busy fending off a soldier. The first he knew of it was when sharp teeth fastened on his arm and shook it, wrenching the ax from his grasp. He cried out in pain and fell backward on one knee.

Briggan snarled, but Abeke was closer. She moved to strike at the wolverine with an arrow, but at the last moment turned her hand to hit it with her fist. It fell away, and she backed off with her eyes and mouth wide.

"Why'd you do that?" asked Conor, clutching his arm and feeling blood pulse under his fingers. He had seen her pull the blow, but why? He fumbled for his ax.

Abeke was looking around her. Suddenly she froze. A lean figure stepped out of the soldiers toward them, a boy not much older than them, but stronger, blonder, and whiter, even under the muck of battle. He caught sight of Abeke, and a flash of recognition went through both of them. Conor, just struggling to his feet with one hand on Briggan's back, saw it clearly. Abeke looked shocked, her dark skin paler than he had ever seen it. The blond boy smiled and raised one hand in greeting.

Abeke was still gaping at him when another enemy soldier brought his sword down toward her head. Conor leaped forward with a yelp, and the blow was blocked by the haft of his ax — and by the thin, curved blade of a saber. Conor's and the blond boy's crossed weapons locked. Abeke blinked into the present and plunged the arrow in her hand deep into the enemy soldier's chest. Briggan jumped at the wolverine, biting savagely as it whipped around to attack again.

With a squeal of steel, the blond boy slowly disengaged his sword, watching Conor the whole time.

"Renneg!" he called, and the wolverine made an odd coughing sound as it retreated.

"Shane," Abeke said.

"Abeke." The blond boy nodded sadly, but he didn't stick around to chat. He backed away and was carried off by the tide of battle.

"Who was that?" panted Conor, swinging his ax to send several enemies scuttling after the boy. "Shane who?"

"None of your business!" snapped Abeke. Her face was flushed, and she was looking at neither Conor nor the retreating boy.

"Ah," said Conor. He had wondered why Abeke had stayed with the Conquerors as long as she had. The handsome boy who had blocked his own soldier's attack to protect Abeke might be that reason.

They had some clear space around them now, with several soldiers withdrawing to follow Shane. A hundred yards away, Conor could see that Tarik, Lishay, Meilin, and Rollan had finally won their way to Dinesh. But the elephant was backing out of the combat, only striking or trampling anyone stupid enough to come after him. As Conor and Abeke pressed forward in hope of joining them, he turned.

"I judge the field to be even now, or close enough. It is for you to carry the day. Or not. I will await the victor."

With that, Dinesh tramped past them, the ground shaking as he went.

The Conquerors stood stunned for a moment as Dinesh retreated, unable to believe their luck. Then they surged forward, hundreds of them charging straight at the Greencloaks and their spirit animals, cutting off Abeke and Conor, with the giant crocodile and its rider coming up fast behind them.

21

A GREAT LOSS

BACK-TO-BACK!" ORDERED TARIK. MEILIN STEPPED INTO place with him, Lishay, and Rollan. Their shoulders touched for a moment, then they found themselves pushed out a little as Meilin released Jhi from her dormant state, the panda suddenly appearing between them. Jhi stood upright, like a column, and they all set their backs against her solid bulk, feeling a wave of rejuvenation radiating out from her. Lumeo crouched between Tarik's feet, but Zhosur snarled and sprang at the first attackers, while Essix tangled in midair with half a dozen enemy birds. Only her superior speed and dexterity saved her from their frenzied attacks.

Within a minute, they were completely surrounded. Meilin whirled her staff almost too fast to be seen, letting well-practiced reflexes guide her blows. Tarik's straight sword flashed and Lishay's curved talwar sang as they cut and hacked at their opponents. Rollan struck with his dagger, quick as Essix falling on a bird. Essix herself dove from above, seeking vulnerable eyes and throats.

But there were too many enemies. Meilin knew it, and she was sure the others did too, although none of them said anything. There wasn't time to talk, and nothing to say anyway. It would only be a matter of minutes before one of them was wounded or killed. This was the end.

Then the enemies around them suddenly surged back, driven away by a charge led by a snorting rhino and a rider stabbing with his lance, and a soldier splendid in crimson and silver, with a badge on his helmet and a sword that shone like liquid silver as it struck. Close behind them were soldiers and rhino riders fighting as if they had trained together for years.

Meilin knew that badge. Her heart leaped on seeing it.

"Father!" she cried.

"Jodoboda!" shouted Rollan.

General Teng saluted Meilin with his sword, then leaped back into the fight, Jodoboda and his rhino at his side. The enemy fell back before them, not expecting this last-minute resurgence. Many threw their weapons away as rhinos ran down their neighbors. The thundering of the mighty animals was as deafening as Dinesh himself.

Meilin leaned back against Jhi, watching her father fight. He was strong and efficient, a beacon of hope in her exhausted state. He kept pace with the rhinos, shouting orders. She longed to follow him, but they needed her there, just as the battle needed General Teng where he was.

Suddenly the giant crocodile and its rider raged through the line of retreating Conquerors, crushing them under clawed foot without care. Jodoboda started to turn his rhino to meet it, but he couldn't get around in time. The huge jaws closed on the rhino's neck, and it fell. Jodoboda clung to the back of his falling beast an instant too long, unwilling to accept its death. Then he let go of the chain and leaped aside. But he fell badly. One leg twisted underneath him, and he did not get up.

The crocodile pushed the dead rhino aside with its ugly snout and advanced on the wearied quartet. The man on its back drew a crescent-shaped blade from the scabbard on his chest and feinted at Tarik, who was closest. Tarik brought his sword up to block it, but the blade flew instead at Lishay, who was also leaning exhausted against Jhi.

She reacted too slowly.

Zhosur leaped even as the blade flew. It struck the tiger with a horrifying thud, sinking deep into the beast's neck. Zhosur fell to the ground at Lishay's feet. The Greencloak cried out, a terrible cry of pain and fear, and dropped to Zhosur's side, clutching the white fur in her fists. Meilin crouched next to her. Perhaps there was something Jhi could do, if they reacted quickly.

But Zhosur had already been bleeding from a dozen lesser wounds before the blade had struck him. Meilin could tell before touching him that he was already dead.

Lishay cried out again, a mournful wail of loss that broke Meilin's heart.

Tarik snarled. She had never heard the Greencloak make so animal a noise before. She looked up in surprise. He was already moving, springing forward, sword raised to strike the mammoth crocodile, but the blow never connected. The crocodile swung its huge armored head, sending him flying through the air to land in a crumpled heap. Lumeo ran after him, chittering in distress.

Meilin sprang to her feet and tried to run to his defense, but Rollan pulled her back, just as the crocodile lunged, its jaws snapping shut in the air where Meilin would have been.

"Beware!" cried a voice she knew well. Her father!

Before the crocodile could attack again, its snout was struck by a flurry of blows from General Teng. Sparks flew from its strange hide, but so did small amounts of blood.

"Meilin, get back!" ordered Teng.

His sword flashed again, knocking another thrown crescent blade aside. The crocodile snapped at him, but he bent over backward, knees bent, one hand to the ground.

The jaws closed on the empty air above him.

Rollan grabbed Meilin around the waist and yanked her away.

"Let me go!" screamed Meilin. "Father!"

She howled as she struggled to extricate herself, determined to help her father, but someone else joined in, pulling her back several steps.

"Too big to fight up close!" said a familiar voice behind her. Meilin whirled around. There was Xue, but this time she had no pack and her back was not bent. She had a sharp chopstick in each hand, and they were bloody. "Find bows, arrows!"

Meilin looked around wildly. She couldn't see any unbroken bows or arrows. But she could see Jodoboda's lance, the end dug into the ground. She ran to it and pulled it out. It was heavy but well balanced, and she was strong.

Rollan had found a bow. He was nocking an arrow too long for it, not very expertly. General Teng dodged another snap of the crocodile's jaws and struck back, causing more sparks to fly, but seemingly doing little else.

"Help me now, Jhi," whispered Meilin. She balanced the lance on her shoulder, gripping it with both hands, and bent her knees, ready to throw it at the crocodile's nearest eye. "It's just like a really sharp piece of bamboo."

Strength and calm flooded into her. She could feel Rollan and Xue at her back, and hear Abeke and Conor running closer, calling. Meilin ignored them all and took a deep breath, balancing carefully on both feet, the lance poised over her right shoulder, every muscle tensed and ready.

At that moment, General Teng slipped on the bloody grass. He recovered almost instantly, bringing up his sword, but not fast enough.

The crocodile's jaws closed powerfully around his body, massive teeth grinding against his armor. He grimaced in terrible pain, but made no sound at all. The sword fell from his hand as he was spat out onto the ground.

Zhongese warriors never cried out in pain. Neither did General Teng or Meilin. Even as the moment of stillness Jhi had given her crumbled under the terrible shock of seeing her father struck down, she chose to act rather than scream.

Putting aside all thought of throwing the lance, Meilin charged.

"Meilin, no!" Rollan was too slow to stop her.

So was the crocodile. It swung its head around to catch the lance in its jaws, but the attempt came too late. The lance struck the corner of its mouth, just above the lip. Driven with all of Meilin's strength as augmented by the Great Beast Jhi, the steel lancehead drove deep into the crocodile's jaw, inflicting a grievous wound.

But not a mortal one.

The crocodile opened its jaws to bite the impudent human who had hurt it so, only to receive Rollan's arrow straight down its gullet. This also was only an annoyance, but its rider saw other archers running up, more Greencloaks with unnatural strength and accuracy.

The crocodile reared up, controlled by the armored man on its back.

"We *will* conquer!" hissed the crocodile's rider. But his actions belied the threat. The crocodile turned and streaked away with astonishing speed, crashing through friends and foes alike.

At that moment, the Conquerors lost the battle. Seeing their general and his great mount retreat, they turned tail and began to flee. Rhino riders ran them down, and the Zhongese gongs began to beat out their shrill command, *Pursue, pursue, pursue!*

Meilin was aware of this only as a distant distraction. She ran to her father and knelt by his side. Blood bubbled from his lips. Impossibly, despite the crushing force of the crocodile's jaws and its huge teeth, the general was still alive!

"Jhi! Jhi!" she called.

The panda pressed in beside her and put one paw on her father's shattered chest. Jhi pressed lightly, then retreated.

"No," called Meilin, reaching out to pull the panda back. "Help him!"

Jhi did not budge. She sat where she was, her stillness indicating there was nothing she could do.

"Meilin."

It was the merest whisper. Meilin put her cheek against her father's, tears trickling down her face.

"Father, I am here."

"I am . . . proud of you, daughter." The words were faint, barely audible over the clash of arms on the battle-field. "Should have told you . . . betrayed . . . the Bile . . ."

He said no more. Meilin felt her father's face go slack under her cheek. Rising up, she saw brown eyes – eyes just like her own – now staring up into an interminable nothing.

The world around her became silent all at once. Meilin lost track of the battlefield. Everything was replaced by a soundless wail – the scream of death. It was so loud. How could they not all hear it? How did they not go mad from it?

Meilin felt Rollan put his hand on her shoulder, and Jhi moved to gently nuzzle her ear. She didn't respond to either of them. Instead, she bent over her father, and gave way to her tears.

It was not true that a Zhongese soldier never cried.

Essix, minus a few feathers, came to land nearby. Conor and Abeke arrived too, but they did not speak. Conor helped a semiconscious Tarik up, and Abeke bent down to see if Lishay was still alive. Uraza nosed at the dead Zhosur and made a small keening noise, deep in her throat.

Meilin rocked back and forth on her knees. She wanted nothing more than to fly like Essix up into the sky and far away from the battlefield. But duty remained, to Jhi and the others, to all of Erdas. The dream of flying was just that, a dream.

She wiped her eyes and stood up.

"The time of the bamboo flowering comes to all," said Xue. "It is the life we lead that matters."

Meilin nodded dumbly, unable to speak. The words were familiar. It was an ancient Zhongese saying. But she had never had them said to her before.

She and her father had come a long way from Jano Rion, thought Meilin. A very long way. Now he at least would never return.

Tarik's hand came down heavily on her shoulder, offering support, even as the battered older Greencloak took it from her as well. The battle had passed on, leaving a trail of dead, wounded, and bereft in its wake. It was strangely quiet, now that all the fighting was in the distance, and moving steadily farther away.

"We've won?" Rollan said.

"For now," said Tarik.

"Lishay's alive," called out Abeke. "But I can't rouse her."

"Do not try," said Xue to Abeke. "To lose a spirit animal is a little death. Some come back. Many do not."

Tarik closed his eyes briefly, as though this was one thing he could not bear.

"So I guess I should go and get the talisman now?" said Rollan. "I mean, in case they come back and counterattack or whatever."

"What do you mean, go and get the talisman?" asked Conor.

"Uh, yeah, that's right. I didn't tell you. It's in the temple. I found it before and . . . er . . . put it back," said Rollan.

"What?!" exclaimed Conor and Abeke in unison.

"Dinesh said that was good! That's why he helped. He said if we won, we could have it . . . so . . ."

"I wondered why Dinesh came to our aid," said Tarik. He bent his head to Rollan. "Truly, Rollan, there's more Greencloak in you than you acknowledge. I hope that you will choose to fully join us, after all."

"Let's not get ahead of ourselves," said Rollan. "Who would you have to lecture at about duty and honor, if I just went and joined up?"

"We'll go get it with you," Meilin spoke with a quiet voice. Her father's body lay broken at her feet. She wasn't ready to be separated from the others yet. They were all she had left.

She held out her hand. Surprised, Rollan took it, and their eyes met. Conor and Abeke hesitated, then joined their hands too, and all four of them looked at each other. They were bloody and exhausted, but they had survived their first major battle against the Devourer. Together.

Jhi watched the proceedings with her silver eyes, and glanced slyly at Briggan. The wolf grinned, his tongue hanging out. Uraza sniffed and began to wash her bloodied paws. Essix, high overhead, issued a long, piercing cry.

22

SLATE ELEPHANT

DINESH RECEIVED THEM AT THE BASE OF THE TUMBLE-
down pyramid with his surviving priests. The Great
Elephant, last seen bleeding from hundreds of small
wounds, now appeared completely unharmed. He was
also somewhat smaller. The priests wore their elephant
heads again, and simple robes of gray, though many also
sported bandages.

"So you have won," said Dinesh. "And you have come
to claim the Slate Elephant."

"We've come to ask for it," said Rollan diplomatically.

"And to thank you for your help," added Abeke.

"I only did what was needed to make it a fair contest,"
rumbled Dinesh. "Maybe a little more, given they had that
huge cold lizard on their side."

"Was it a Great Beast?" asked Conor. "The crocodile?
Like our spirit animals were?"

"Oh, no, child," said Dinesh. "We Great Beasts are sib-
lings of a sort. Though it is long since I knew the doings

of the others, we are all stewards of Erdas, to the last of us. Even Kovo and Gerathon, in their folly. No other creatures, great as they may become, can ever become a Great Beast. Still, that spirit animal and its rider do bear a striking resemblance. . . ."

"I am fairly sure that was General Gar," said Abeke. "Though I couldn't see his face."

"There is no doubt now that the Devourer has returned," said Tarik gravely. "As we feared."

"Whether he is the Devourer or not, you must go from here soon," said Dinesh. "The Conquerors have suffered a defeat, but there are many more of them coming. They have found or made a way through the Great Bamboo Maze, and no part of Pharsit Nang is safe. They will attack again, and soon. I myself will be seeking a quieter place to continue my contemplations."

"We'll go back with the rhino riders to begin with, if they will take us." Tarik turned to Jodoboda, who stood with them, his leg splinted and his arm around the shoulders of one of his riders for support. His beard was filthy, and he wore the heavy chain of his fallen rhino around his neck, as a sign of mourning.

"We will take you," said Jodoboda. "The Zhongese resistance too. We've decided we will fight the Conquerors together in Pharsit Nang, just as you have counseled all this time, Old Mother," he added to Xue. "As always, you have gotten your way!"

"You mean you found your good sense," said Xue with a snort.

"Thanks from us too," said Rollan to Jodoboda. "We would've been lost without the rhinos, and Meilin's father . . . and your priests too, Dinesh."

"All were needed," said Dinesh with a heavy sigh, as though resigning himself to a loss no less painful than Meilin's. "And all did what was needful. Go get the talisman. It is yours to wield now."

Rollan sketched a hasty but sincere bow, and went off at a run to climb the higgledy-piggledy steps of the pyramid, Essix flying in loops over his head.

When he returned, it was to silence, the silence of exhaustion. They had won a battle and gained the Slate Elephant, but it was at a terrible cost. What would the quest for the next talisman demand of them?

"Whose talisman will you seek next?" asked Dinesh. "What Great Beast will have their solitude pierced by your grasping little voices?"

"We do not know," said Tarik.

"Unless you want to help us again," said Abeke. "You mentioned something about Suka being entombed in ice. Where was that exactly?"

Dinesh laughed, a deep rumble that echoed across the crater.

"Somewhere cold," he said, his eyes twinkling. "I can say no more. Somewhere very cold."

"That'll make a welcome change," said Rollan, holding up the chain with the Slate Elephant slowly circling on the end for all to see. "I've got it."

"Just don't give it away," said Conor.

Rollan was unsure for a moment whether Conor was joking or not. But of course he was. He had to be.

"We've *done* that," Rollan said. "Let's not make that our thing."

Uraza suddenly growled and hissed at something behind them.

Everyone turned to look. Lishay was lying on a stretcher nearby. Her wounds had been tended, but she still had not woken. Her cheeks were hollow, and her long hair was unbound.

Now, a tiger with black stripes was sitting by Lishay's head, making mewling noises and batting at her face with a velvet paw, the claws retracted.

Uraza started forward, but Abeke raised her hand, and the leopard stopped. Rollan watched in wonder.

The black tiger let out a mournful yowl and began to lick Lishay's cheek. The Greencloak turned her head and mumbled something, throwing out her arm, the fingers lightly grasping the fur on the tiger's back.

"Zhosur?" she said, slightly raising her head. Her eyes opened and she saw her slain twin brother's spirit animal. "Zhamin?"

The tiger purred and bent his head. Lishay sobbed and wrapped her arms around the tiger, which promptly vanished in a flash of light.

Lishay slowly pushed up her right sleeve and then her left, staring at the tattoos of leaping tigers, one on each forearm. The left one was a white tiger, but it was faded, as if made by a ghost. The other, vibrant and new, showed a tiger as black as a starless night.

"Never seen *that* before," said Xue.